"Don't go," Kyle murmured

She'd never heard her friend's voice sound so husky before, not even when he was sick with the flu. It was sexy husky, we-just-made-love-all-night-long husky. It made her shiver.

He pulled on her arm, urging her down. His hand encircling her wrist felt warm. "Stay. Stay here, Mel. Come back."

"I..." She didn't want to get into this now. She didn't want a scene. She'd wanted to disappear quietly.

"Stay," he repeated.

He pulled harder. She went. It happened so smoothly, so seamlessly. He turned her onto her side, facing outward, and curled his big, warm body around hers, spoon style. He clamped an arm around her waist. He buried his face in the back of her neck, nuzzling her there, kissing her nape.

"Your hair..." Kyle inhaled deeply. "Smells like gardenia. Mmm. Melissa. I just want to hold you," he said drowsily.

The words undid her. Without her conscious volition, her eyelids fluttered shut. And then contentment seeped through her limbs.

She couldn't help it. She didn't want to. It felt too good.

But even as she let herself drift back to sleep, part of her knew this was wrong.

Kyle. Oh, Kyle. What have

Dear Reader,

Kyle and Melissa, the hero and heroine of this book, have known each other several years when their relationship changes suddenly and irrevocably. I've always had a soft spot for stories like theirs, stories about close friends who fall in love—with a little help from external circumstances.

Maybe the two people have been in love all along but for various reasons haven't been able to admit it. Or maybe an unexpected situation forces them to see each other in a new light. Regardless, the developing romance between longtime friends can be particularly complex.

True, "love at first sight" is very powerful. But there's also something powerful about really *knowing* the other person before you fall in love—knowing his or her strengths and weaknesses and having more access to the inner layers of his or her personality. Within that context, a couple's interactions take on new—and sometimes richer— meanings.

In Melissa and Kyle's story I've tried to capture some of that emotional depth. This book is very different in tone from anything else I've written (including my new Harlequin American Romance novel). I hope you enjoy my efforts!

Anne Haven

BECAUSE
OF
THE
BABY
Anne
Haven

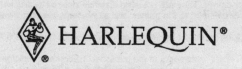

HARLEQUIN®

TORONTO • NEW YORK • LONDON
AMSTERDAM • PARIS • SYDNEY • HAMBURG
STOCKHOLM • ATHENS • TOKYO • MILAN • MADRID
PRAGUE • WARSAW • BUDAPEST • AUCKLAND

ISBN 0-373-70905-6

BECACAUSE OF THE BABY

BECAUSE OF THE BABY

Visit us at www.romance.net

Printed in U.S.A.

To Ruth—with boundless gratitude for your
hard work and support

PROLOGUE

Midsummer

MELISSA LOPEZ AWOKE in the unfamiliar bed with the unfamiliar weight of an arm slung over her rib cage. Long white muslin curtains billowed in from an open window nearby. Bright morning sunshine poured into the room, making her squint. She gazed straight above her, blinking as her eyes adjusted.

High ceiling with exposed ductwork and a bumpy, texturized white finish that looked like cottage cheese.

Not her ceiling.

Oh, God. Oh, good God Almighty. *Kyle's ceiling. Kyle's bed. Kyle's big, tanned, muscular arm draped over her naked torso.*

A crisp white sheet covered them. Melissa felt the warmth from his body all along her right side. His bent knee rested against her leg, the curling hairs tickling her skin. She sensed his head on the pillow beside her, heard the even cadence of his breath and became aware of its caress against her ear and neck.

Slowly she turned her head. Kyle Davenport lay asleep on his side, facing her. His long, dark lashes rested peacefully against his cheeks.

His lips were full and slightly darker than usual and a day's beard growth shadowed his jaw. He had short hair, a faintly crooked nose, high cheekbones and a strong, attractive chin. He looked like himself—though she wasn't used to this vantage point.

She swallowed. *The vantage point of lying next to him. In bed.*

Again she thought, Oh, God.

Images flashed in her mind. His apartment at night. The whisper of clothing as it slid off their skin. Warm, wet, breathless kisses. Hands exploring. His and hers.

She'd never touched him before. Never like last night. She'd only looked—looked and tried not to see his masculine beauty. Tried not to want.

I don't believe what we did.

She'd needed him last night. After what had happened in the E.R. she'd been desperate. A small child and his mother had come in, fresh from a car accident. The boy had looked so much like Melissa's brother. Same age. Similar injuries. And this boy had died, too. Melissa hadn't been able to save him. Informing his mother—

Usually she was able to maintain a doctor's professional distance. Last night she hadn't.

So, when her shift at the E.R. had ended, she'd

turned to Kyle. She'd needed the solace he could give her and she hadn't cared about anything else.

But they should not have become lovers. She and Kyle couldn't be romantically involved. They had a very good, very comfortable friendship—and this was a sure way to mess it up. She valued their relationship too much to let it degenerate into another of Kyle's light, temporary affairs.

Panic shot through her.

She had to get away.

Her pulse hammering, Melissa raised a hand to his arm. He didn't stir as she painstakingly eased his arm off her torso and inched away from him, pausing once when the mattress creaked. She lowered a leg over the side of the bed.

Kyle caught her wrist as she started to rise. "Don't go," he murmured.

She'd never heard his voice so husky before, not even when he was sick with the flu. It was sexy husky, we-just-made-love-all-night-long husky. It made her shiver.

He pulled on her arm, urging her down. His hand, encircling her wrist, felt warm. "Stay. Stay here, Mel. Come back."

"I..." She didn't want to get into this now. She didn't want a scene. She'd wanted to disappear quietly.

"Stay," he repeated.

He pulled harder. She went. It happened so smoothly, so seamlessly. He turned her onto her side, facing outward, and curled his big, warm body around hers, spoon style. He clamped an arm around her waist. He buried his face in the back of her neck, nuzzling her there, kissing her nape.

"Your hair..." Kyle inhaled deeply. "Smells like gardenia. Mmm. Melissa. I just want to hold you," he said drowsily.

The words undid her. Without her conscious volition, her eyelids fluttered shut. And then contentment seeped through her limbs.

She couldn't help it. She didn't want to. It felt too good.

But even as she let herself drift back to sleep, part of her knew this was wrong. Terribly.

Kyle. Oh, Kyle. What have we done?

CHAPTER ONE

October

KYLE DAVENPORT STARED at the pasty-faced, middle-aged man in front of him. They sat in the makeshift conference corner of his office, on a pair of scuffed metal folding chairs pulled up to a Formica-topped table salvaged from a diner. Boxes of medical supplies and free samples lined the shelves on the wall beside them.

Kyle clasped his hands on the tabletop. As the clinic's director he usually spent more time on his administrative duties than he did interacting with patients, but he welcomed the chance to do so. Even when, like today, he had to play the heavy.

"Harry," he said. "Sounds like we have a problem here. Barbara tells me you haven't been taking your meds."

The man gave him a cranky look. He brushed back a chunk of his badly cut gray hair and then inspected the fingerless wool gloves he wore. "Barbara's a bully."

"She only wants to help you get better. If you

don't take your meds, Harry, you won't get better.''

"I hate the meds."

"I know. I'd hate taking 'em, too. But it's the only way to make you improve. And if you don't take 'em you'll probably get worse. Keep this up and you'll end up in the hospital.''

They both knew Harry had no health coverage, which was why he came to the free clinic. He couldn't afford another emergency-room visit like the one last spring. He hadn't been able to afford *that* one.

"Harry, help me out here. I know it's a pain in the ass to take 'em three times a day. But Barbara can't do anything for you if you ignore everything she says.''

"She says too much. She's always on my back. I'm going to start calling her Nurse Ratched.''

Kyle tried not to grin, knowing he shouldn't encourage the guy. But he couldn't wait to tell Barbara about her new nickname. "I don't think that'll increase her level of friendliness, Harry.'' He flattened his palms on the table and adopted a serious tone. "Look, buddy, I really need you to take those pills. Why don't you try it for a week and we'll take the rest as it comes, okay?''

Harry shot him a defiant glare. "The meds,'' he announced, "give me gas.''

Kyle raised his eyebrows. "Oh, do they, now? Well, I can't say I'd like that, either… It's bad?''

"You don't want to know." And that, apparently, settled the matter. Harry grasped the edge of the table and supported himself as he rose to his feet. He adjusted the ragged old tweed coat he wore 365 days a year, rain or shine, heat or snow. "Well. Guess I'll be going now."

Kyle stood, too. "Hey, not so fast. I just had an idea. Hear me out?"

The other man turned back, head tilted, expression doubtful.

"There might be a solution," Kyle said. "We'd have to talk to Barbara, but it might be possible to change your prescription. We could try to find something that isn't so hard on your system."

"Like what?"

"I don't know. I'm not a nurse or doctor. But sometimes more than one med can treat the same problem."

Harry had his new bottle of meds by the time Melissa arrived for her weekly shift as a volunteer physician at the clinic. Through the doorway of his office Kyle heard Melissa greet Harry by name and the older man give her a cheerful, flirtatious response before leaving the clinic.

Kyle tried to focus on his paperwork. He had plenty this week, and a long list of phone calls to make for the fall fund-raising drive.

But he couldn't concentrate. Never could on Wednesday afternoons, not since a certain hot summer night in July. He got that familiar, socked-in-the-gut feeling he had whenever he remembered it. Melissa, he thought, would be in to say hello any second.

Right on cue, she stuck her head through the doorway. "Hey, Kyle. How's it going today?"

She wore her long white coat and a stethoscope looped around her neck. She always pulled her chocolate-brown hair back in a clasp at her nape; a few strands had escaped to graze her jaw. In one hand she held a clipboard; in the other, a half-eaten apple.

He smiled, knowing his face looked just as friendly and calm and unruffled as hers. "Great. Not too busy with the walk-ins. You've got some appointments?"

She glanced down at the clipboard. "That's right." She raised an eyebrow. "Mmm. I see Zita is scheduled for a visit. That should be colorful."

Zita, a.k.a. Susan Smith, was a recovering addict with a variety of physical ailments caused by years of hard living. She had an eccentric personality and a loud voice.

"And a couple of new ones..." Melissa crunched on a bite of apple as she skimmed the notes. "Okay." She swallowed and looked up at him.

"How's your week going?" Kyle asked.

"Fine." Her eyes met his and held them, but not for too long. Just long enough to show them both that everything was normal, routine, mundane, unremarkable. As it had been for the past five years. Just long enough to prove they weren't avoiding eye contact. "My high-school chem teacher turned up in the E.R. last night."

"Nothing serious, I hope."

She shook her head. "Only a sprained ankle. Thought it might have been broken, but he was lucky. It was nice to talk to him—I hadn't seen the man since graduation fifteen years ago."

Melissa, an exceptionally bright and hardworking student, had finished high school at sixteen. She'd enrolled at Harvard med school three years later. Kyle had always found her intelligence incredibly sexy.

He took a deep breath. It's none of your business, he told himself, whether she's sexy or not. You're just friends. That's all you've ever been.

Except that crazy night in July.

But that had been a mistake. An aberration. They'd each had reasons for letting it happen— fine. But now they'd moved on. Put things back to normal.

A moment later Melissa tossed her apple core into the trash and went off to see to her patients. Kyle forced his attention back to his paperwork and phone calls.

He'd been running the health clinic, designed to serve the homeless and low-income population of Portland, Oregon, since he'd moved out west six years ago. Needing a change of scene. Needing to get away from all the memories of Felicity.

It had taken awhile to adjust. He'd had experience in nonprofits, but twenty-six had been young for this kind of position. Yet he'd thrown himself into the job, welcoming the challenge and the distraction. He'd barely had a personal life that first year, but he hadn't wanted one—he'd found it almost intolerable to interact with anyone when it wasn't part of his job.

Kyle remembered all the nights he'd gone home to his empty apartment, unable even to summon the energy to feed himself dinner before collapsing, still clothed, into bed. Welcoming the blankness of sleep.

But things had gotten better. He'd emerged from that brooding, self-pitying year and started to recapture his old self. Back in Boston, before Felicity's suicide, he'd always been a social, fun-loving guy. He'd made new friends in Portland and begun to date again. Not seriously, of course—Felicity's death had cured him of any impulse to get serious—but he'd learned to enjoy himself once more. And then Melissa had become a volunteer at the clinic.

Their friendship had evolved. She'd been wary at first, and had quickly made it clear she wouldn't be one of his conquests. Relationships that involved sex or romance, he'd noticed, scared the devil out of her. She certainly didn't want a dalliance—which was all he was prepared to offer.

So their acquaintance had taken a different route. They'd respected each other's differences and limitations and boundaries, and gradually, without any intent, they'd developed the unlikeliest of friendships.

No, they didn't tell each other everything. But sometimes they didn't have to. Sometimes they just understood each other.

And sometimes, he suspected, they just kept secrets—from the world and themselves and each other.

SIX O'CLOCK ARRIVED before he could finish his work. It always did. He needed an assistant, but the clinic couldn't afford one, so he made do with occasional volunteer help. This month they were short on volunteers.

Barbara Purcell, the large, attractive, forty-five-year-old black woman who served as the clinic's nurse practitioner, walked into the room and snatched the papers from his hands. "That's it. It's closing time, boy. I'm hungry, Melissa's hungry and that perky little college-girl receptionist is hungry." She tapped the papers on the desktop to straighten them, then laid them down on a corner of the surface. Just out of his reach.

Kyle didn't bother to protest. Three hungry women—especially *these* three hungry women,

none of whom deprived themselves of daily nour-
ishment to attain an impossible female ideal—were
more than he could go up against. Not to mention
he was hungry himself.

"Thi's Pho Shop?" he said.

Barbara gave him a who-stole-your-brain look.
"Where else?"

The four of them collected in the waiting area a
couple of minutes later. They locked up and
headed down the street, laughing and groaning,
complaining and elbow-ribbing, a close-knit, ani-
mated group.

The restaurant, which served nothing but beef
noodle soup, stood at the corner. It was always
packed with Vietnamese Americans during the first
half of the day, as traditionally *pho* was eaten for
breakfast and lunch.

This evening the shop hummed with a mixed
clientele. The proprietor's daughter, a teenager in
combat boots, jeans and a plaid flannel shirt, led
them to a table by the window.

"Nice spot," Melissa commented, taking the
seat beside his. "In fact, it's the nicest spot in the
restaurant." She winked at him. "I think that girl's
got a crush on you, Kyle."

Whitney, the college student who worked several afternoons as the clinic's receptionist, rolled
her eyes. "Every straight female he meets gets a
crush on him." She reached for some napkins and

spoons and chopsticks from the dispenser on the table.

"Hey, I'm straight," Barbara said.

"Me, too." Melissa looked at him, tilting her head in feigned sympathy. She patted his shoulder. "Sorry, Kyle. We can't all join your mass of admirers."

Everyone laughed, aware of Kyle's undeniably sexy good looks.

The waitress brought them ice water and took their orders. After she left, Kyle steered the conversation to a different topic. He told himself it wasn't because he minded Melissa's teasing. But he felt edgy and a little raw tonight.

Melissa had spoken about his interactions with women the way she always had. She'd been tolerant, amused, occasionally chiding. Nothing had changed. His love life didn't affect her. Yet he wondered how she could act that way so easily after what they'd done last July.

Damn it, Kyle. You should be grateful she's handling it like this and not flipping out. Not getting all needy and emotional. Not trying to rope you into a heavy-duty commitment.

Their bowls of *pho* arrived.

"Oh, yes." Barbara closed her eyes and inhaled the ambrosial aroma of beef stock rich with onions and ginger and star anise. "Sometimes I dream about this soup."

"No kidding." Melissa added bean sprouts and

fresh herbs from the condiment plate, then a drizzle of lime. "Mmm. I might just have to have seconds tonight."

AFTER THE MEAL Barbara drove home to her daughter and son-in-law. Whitney, like Kyle, had taken the bus to the clinic that day, so Melissa gave her a ride to Reed College before heading for his apartment.

Every Wednesday night after Melissa's volunteer shift and the group dinner, they went to his apartment and watched *X-Files* reruns. The pattern hadn't changed since the summer. It hadn't changed since they'd made love.

They'd gone to bed together, shared a night of mind-blowing sex and then miraculously gone back to business as usual.

With anyone but Melissa it would have been absurd. Unthinkable. But she had a way of making it seem like the natural thing to do.

Pretend it didn't happen. Ignore it. It doesn't really exist, this knowledge of what we did together, of the tastes and textures of each other's bodies; we don't really know that.

We're just friends. Best friends, yes. But nothing more.

Melissa parked her car, a safe, dependable white sedan, outside his apartment building. Two years ago she'd moved with her sister into a little house around the corner; she wouldn't have to drive again until morning.

They entered the lobby and stopped by the bank of metal mailboxes, discussing some clients at the clinic. Just as they usually did. They took the stairs instead of the elevator to his third-floor, one-bedroom apartment, as usual.

Kyle let her in. He tossed his black leather bag onto the dining-room table, thumbed through his mail and tossed it down, too.

The answering machine said he had two messages. He played them back as he opened the fridge and grabbed a beer for himself and filtered water for Melissa. One of the calls was from a professional contact, the other from his mother in Massachusett.

"Haven't phoned her in two weeks, hmm? Tsk, tsk." Melissa pulled out a bag of gingersnaps from a kitchen cabinet. "Better shape up, Kyle."

"Yeah, I know. I'll give her a ring tomorrow, promise. I'm sure she's already in bed by now. It's after ten out there."

He also ought to talk with his brother soon, but Craig was a little harder to reach. No doubt they would catch each other over the weekend.

He and Melissa carried their drinks into the living room, a contemporary space with simple yet cozy furniture. Melissa had helped him decorate the room, suggesting rusty browns and muted greens—subtle, earthy colors—to go with the pale walls and carpet. A huge ficus tree, which survived only because she remembered to check it regularly, stood in a corner by one of the large windows.

Kyle set her water on the coffee table and sprawled on the couch with his beer.

She sat a couple feet away from him, opening the bag of gingersnaps as she kicked off her shoes. She gave his knee a nudge with her sock-clad foot. "Don't take your mother for granted, Kyle. She's the only one you've got."

"I know."

Melissa had lost hers years ago. When she'd been eight, her mother and five-year-old brother had died in the emergency room following a car accident. She'd been the only other person in the car with them when they'd collided with a truck. Kyle didn't think she'd ever gotten over the fact that she'd lived and they hadn't, though it wasn't something she talked about.

Her sister, who was one year older than she, had been at a baseball game with their father. They'd lived on, just as Melissa had, but not very well. Her father had become depressed and Anita hadn't fared so well, either. Melissa had tried to take care of them, even though she was the youngest. She still did.

Kyle doubted they still wanted or needed her to, however.

Last July Anita had decided to get an apartment with her boyfriend. It was a big deal. The sisters had lived together for years, ever since Melissa had returned to Portland after med school. Melissa, he knew, had liked sharing a household. But Anita, at thirty-two, had wanted to live away from family members—something she'd never done before. She'd made her announcement right before that crazy, unexpected night in July...

The X-Files came on. Kyle took a swig from his beer bottle and tried to concentrate on the show. In his peripheral vision he saw Melissa tuck her feet up under her on the couch and nibble on her gingersnaps.

The episode was one of their favorites, but it didn't hold his attention. Melissa did.

Whitney at the clinic had once told him his relationship with Melissa was like the one between the *X-Files'* main characters, FBI agents Mulder and Scully. He'd laughed. But the comparison had some validity, he acknowledged to himself. He and Melissa had the same kind of connection, a quiet respect and unwavering loyalty to each other. They trusted each other with their lives, though they rarely discussed their innermost feelings.

And the sexual tension. It was always there in the background, simmering. Neither of them would admit it, but that was how it was.

After the show ended, Melissa picked up the remote from the coffee table and switched off the television. "You okay, Kyle?"

"Mmm, sure."

"You seem a little distracted." Reaching back, she patted her hair and felt that it had gotten mussed. She released the tortoiseshell clasp and ran her fingers through the straight strands.

The movements weren't intended to be seductive. They *were* seductive, though, and it didn't help his distractedness.

I did that, he thought. *I ran my fingers through that hair, felt its silken texture. I know it smells like gardenia.*

He'd caught himself leaning too close to her recently, trying to get a whiff.

It made it worse, he thought, to know what she smelled like, felt like, tasted like. Now that he'd seen her naked body, caressed her curves, it had become almost torturous to be near her.

Especially to be near her and not be able to do it all again.

He swallowed. "Guess I'm a little preoccupied with the fall fund drive," he said. A fib. He hated to lie to her and he didn't have much practice. The need had never arisen in the past. But she wouldn't want to hear about him lusting after her. "Sorry."

"Anything I can do to help?"

"Nah. You're already volunteering plenty." Kyle finished off his beer, which was flat and warm. He decided he'd better attempt some kind of conversation. Assure them both everything was okay. "So…any luck finding a roommate this week?"

Anita had moved out of their little house around the corner on September 1st. More than a month had passed and somehow none of Melissa's roommate applicants had worked out yet.

She shook her head. "Actually, I've been thinking of calling off the search. Living by myself for a while."

He gave her a look. "Because you think she'll come running back," he said, and they both knew he meant Anita.

"Honestly? Yes."

"What if she doesn't?"

"Then I'll live alone." She gave a half smile, just a slight quirk of the lips. "Maybe it'll be good for me."

"You know how I feel about that." It would be great for her. He'd been telling her so for years. She needed to live for herself awhile, instead of for others.

"Then why are you eyeing me as if I've done something wrong?" she said.

Okay, they weren't going to have a lighthearted conversation tonight. This would be one of their serious ones, instead. That was fine, he told himself. As long as it didn't pertain to the two of them. "You're not planning to live alone. You're planning for your poor, weak, flighty sister to have a dramatic breakup with her boyfriend, just like she always does, and then come running back to you. You're counting on it. She probably knows it."

"Am I supposed to expect their relationship to last? Expect her and Ty—"

"Troy," he corrected.

"Troy." She paused. "I'm supposed to expect them to live happily ever after? That's never happened before."

"How many times has your sister moved in with a guy?" He knew the answer, but he wanted her to say it.

"Never. But she's talked this way about plenty of guys. I can always recognize it. She gets the same tone in her voice, the same look in her eyes. You want to know what it says? 'It's real this time. He's my knight in shining armor. He's the one who's going to sweep me off my feet and make everything all right.' But it never lasts."

"Maybe this time is different."

"It's not." She spoke with absolute certainty.

Kyle considered her. "Okay. Say it isn't. Say the relationship goes up in smoke. You really think it's good for her to come running back to you?"

"Who else can she turn to?"

She didn't say, *Not my father. I'm the only strong one in the family.* She didn't have to. He'd heard her say it in so many ways a hundred times before.

"Mel, what about her standing on her own two feet? Not needing to depend on anyone?"

"You sound like such a *guy*, Kyle. All that independent, rugged-individualist stuff." She stood up. Grabbed his beer bottle and her water glass and the gingersnaps. "In my family," she said, "we support one another when times are tough."

Melissa carried her load to the kitchen. She returned with a cloth and wiped up the three microscopic cookie crumbs she'd gotten on the coffee table. Her hair clasp, which she'd set on the arm of the couch, went neatly into her pocket.

He knew she didn't realize how revealing her actions were. She'd spoken so calmly, but that obviously wasn't how she felt.

She always cleaned things when she was agitated. Tidied a pile of papers. Dusted a picture frame. Suddenly remembered a load of laundry that needed to be folded.

She bunched up the cloth in her hand, spotted a coffee mug he'd left on the end table yesterday and walked over to get it. When she turned around, the most direct route to the kitchen was between the couch and the coffee table. She took a few steps forward.

He didn't think. He just raised a leg, resting his foot on the side of the coffee table, barring her path.

"Kyle—"

She faced him. Their gazes locked. Something hot and electric and impossible passed between them.

"Kyle, move." She didn't step over his leg. His bent knee reached the level of her thighs; she would have had to straddle him. But she didn't pivot and go the other way, either.

He ached to tumble her onto the couch, on top of him. To kiss her again. He ignored the urge. He looked up at her and said, "What about you, Melissa? Who do *you* lean on when times are tough?"

Her gaze wavered, sliding sideways. She towered over him, spine straight, the cloth in one hand and the mug in the other, and didn't give him an answer.

"Come on, tell me. I want to know. Who takes care of *you?* Who do *you* turn to?"

She shook her head. "Stop it."

He couldn't. Suddenly he couldn't stop himself. It had been building in him for two and a half months, he finally acknowledged. This restless, edgy energy. This urge to push against her emotionally, to shake things up and break things down, even though he knew he shouldn't. Even though it could screw up their friendship.

"Or is that just for other people?" he demanded. "For the weak ones?"

"Don't."

"I need to know the answer."

"You already know it."

"I do? Because it doesn't seem that way to me."

"Damn it, Kyle." She glared down at him.

He blinked. Hell, it looked as if she had tears in her eyes. Oh, God. He'd made her cry. He was being a jerk and he wasn't even sure what he was saying.

Remorse and shame flooded through him. He dropped his foot to the floor. He raised his hands and pressed them to his forehead, a weary gesture.

"I'm sorry," he said. "I didn't mean to be such an ass. I'm not myself right now."

He heard Melissa sit down next to him and sensed the couch shifting beneath her weight.

For a moment she was silent. Then, "Me, neither." The words came out as a whisper.

Kyle wanted to take her in his arms right then. He wanted to comfort her, even though he didn't know all the reasons she might need comforting.

But he held himself back. She had her boundaries. He had to respect them. And she *did* accept his support in other ways. She did turn to him when times were tough.

He wasn't prepared when she spoke again. He hadn't expected anymore from her. But she gave it to him, and it was more than he'd ever imagined.

"I'm pregnant," she said.

CHAPTER TWO

MELISSA HAD NEVER felt an earthquake before. Now she knew what it would be like.

It would begin as a distant rumble; you couldn't be sure it was real. Just a slight, subtle hum. But then you would start to feel the vibrations. You would realize the floor was shaking beneath your feet, the walls were shaking, the furniture was shaking.

And the noise—that unearthly rumble growing louder and louder, gaining textures, piling up on itself, creaking, shifting, shuddering and shattering. A cacophony of sound.

The books in the shelf near the TV, she thought, would tumble to the floor. The framed paintings on the walls would rattle and hang askew. Or slide down the wall, hit the floor with a bang. Plaster and paint would flake from the ceiling.

Then suddenly the earthquake would be over, gone more quickly than it had come. Leaving behind a deafening silence.

She looked at Kyle, sitting quietly beside her on the couch, his forehead buried in his hands. He hadn't moved. An emotional earthquake had passed through his living room and he hadn't moved.

He didn't even glance up. Rubble lay all around them—the rubble of their lives as they'd known them, their lives before this moment.

Before they'd made love.

Before she'd told him the truth.

Before he'd known they'd made a baby together.

Melissa set the mug and washcloth down on the coffee table. "Kyle, please. Say something."

He dropped his hands from his forehead and looked over at her. For a long moment he didn't speak. They just stared at each other, trying to read thoughts through eyes. To understand emotions without words.

"You're pregnant," he finally said.

"Yes."

"From that night in July."

He didn't need her confirmation. Of course he knew it couldn't be otherwise. She didn't exactly have a highly active sex life. At thirty-one, she'd had fewer partners than most eighteen-year-olds.

Kyle massaged his temples. "I can't believe this. We used protection. We were careful."

"No, we weren't," she said.

If they'd been careful they never would have made love at all. She saw by his expression he knew what she meant.

But they hadn't been their normal selves that night. They'd each been running from something, each seeking a way to forget. And their solution had worked—temporarily.

Now they had to face the consequences of their foolishness.

"Condoms aren't one hundred percent effective," she reminded him.

"I know. But I never thought—" He stopped, shaking his head. "How long have you known?"

This was the part she'd dreaded. She didn't want to tell him. She couldn't explain or justify her behavior. "About—about six weeks."

"Jesus, Mel. That long?"

"I wanted to tell you sooner. I just—couldn't." She felt overwhelmed. Overstimulated. As if she were having one of her sister's anxiety attacks. She took a deep, calming breath and forced tense muscles to release and relax. "I'm sorry."

She stared straight ahead at the blank television. Kyle had a twenty-five-inch screen—almost double the size of hers—which was why they always watched *The X-Files* at his place.

"It was right after my birthday," she said. "I'm not…very regular, so it took me a while to figure it out."

"You haven't been getting sick or anything. I would have noticed if you'd started throwing up every day."

"Of course. But not all pregnant women experience morning sickness."

"Oh."

She could feel his gaze on her.

We're going to have a baby.

It was a thought she'd had many times recently. She would look over at him as they were working, or driving somewhere, or sharing a meal, and she would know she had to tell him. But the words had always refused to come. Her tongue had felt heavy and thick and incapable of forming the right sounds. She'd let the moments pass.

Until tonight.

"I don't understand this," Kyle said. "I don't understand how you could—" He waved a hand in the air, momentarily speechless. His gaze pinned hers. "How could you act so normal? All this time. Six weeks, for God's sake, you've known you're carrying our baby."

Melissa abruptly grabbed the items she'd set on the coffee table. She stood and headed for the kitchen.

Kyle followed her.

She wiped down the counters, loaded a few more items into the dishwasher. A butter knife. The bowl and spoon Kyle had used for his cereal that morning.

He stood and watched her, leaning a hip against the edge of the counter, arms crossed. "You asked me to say something back there. Now it's your turn. Talk to me, Mel."

She stopped and closed her eyes, flattening both

hands on the countertop. "I don't know if I'm ready," she admitted.

"It's been six weeks since you found out. How much more time do you need?"

More than I've gotten. A lifetime, maybe. I'm simply not prepared for this.

"You weren't even going to tell me tonight, were you?"

She shook her head. "It was just because you... said what you did," she admitted.

She stared down at the backs of her hands. Doctor's hands. Well trained, sensitive yet strong. A narrow scar ran from her left wrist toward her thumb, a memento from that day over twenty years ago. And she had other scars, too—the invisible kind. The kind that wrenched you from sleep in the middle of the night, soaked with the sweat from another bad dream.

"How long were you going to wait, then?" Kyle asked. "Until you started to show? Were you going to make me work it out on my own when I saw your belly get big?"

She turned toward him, chin raised. "Kyle, I can't do this right now. I need some space."

He ran a hand through his short, dark hair, tousling it.

The man was gorgeous, she thought—an irrelevant, inappropriate fact to focus on. But she didn't stop herself. She let herself stare at the father of her baby.

The firm, lean muscles of his tall physique attested to the hours he spent on the basketball court at the park down the street; to the long runs and summer hikes and that intense kind of yoga he did.

He held himself and moved with graceful, careless elegance; easy charm. And unutterably sexy masculinity. Two and a half months ago Melissa had lost her ability to ignore it.

She remembered what it had been like to make love with him. He'd been very, very good in bed, drawing out her arousal until she'd lost control. Until she'd whimpered and moaned in a way that embarrassed and appalled her now.

She turned away so he wouldn't see the flush spreading over her ears and face.

He sighed. "I'll walk you home."

"Thank you."

He always walked her around the corner after dark. Their urban neighborhood wasn't a bad one, but Kyle said he saw no point in taking chances. He liked to make sure she got home safely.

Kyle had an intensely protective side, and because she knew him, she didn't think it was sexist. Just caring. In his own way—despite his fear of commitment, his inability to sustain a long-term romantic relationship—Kyle was very caring.

He did good work at the clinic, touching hundreds of lives.

He loved his mother and his younger brother and had looked after them when his father had decided to drop out of the family, leaving only a mildly apologetic note and a pile of overdue bills.

And he'd loved Felicity. The woman who, despite her name, had been hopelessly, hopelessly sad. Too sad to stay in the world, even with Kyle right beside her. Even when their wedding date had been only three weeks away.

In silence she and Kyle walked downstairs and left the apartment building. The night air had a hint of fall crispness and she was glad for the light sweater she wore. Beside her Kyle shoved his hands in his pockets and strolled along, looking almost like his usual, easygoing self.

How many people, she wondered, would guess what kind of conversation they'd just had? Who would think, seeing their composed expressions and unexceptional behavior, that they'd discussed, for the very first time, the new life they'd created together?

Briefly she stared upward at a dark, cloudless sky dotted with thousands of glittering pinpricks of light. So many, many stars. And they were so far away her mind couldn't even begin to grasp the distance. She marveled at the vastness of the universe the way a child would.

In such a big space as the universe, she was small, and insignificant in the grand scheme of things, but she existed.

I'm right here with Kyle. Kyle Davenport, my best friend.

And by midspring our baby will be with us, too.

Our baby. The phrase still had the power to shock her. Even after six weeks she couldn't quite believe she was pregnant.

Barely aware of her actions, she cupped the faint curve of her abdomen.

"No one else knows?" Kyle asked as they turned the corner onto her street.

"No."

"You could have told your sister."

Melissa grasped his meaning. She could have told Anita and gotten her to move back in. It would have been the perfect way. Her sister would have come back to help her throughout the pregnancy. But then, Anita would have been the one taking care of *her*. And it was supposed to be the other way around, wasn't it?

Maybe Kyle was right. Maybe that *was* why she hadn't told her sister yet. She couldn't stand to be the one in trouble, the one who might need support.

"There's a lot we'll have to discuss," Kyle said.

"I know."

"You should let me know when you're ready to tell other people. I won't do it until you're ready, but we should both tell our families soon. You *are* going to keep the baby, I assume."

"Yes. Yes, of course."

They both understood she could never have an abortion, even though she believed in a woman's right to choose.

"How much time do you think you'll need?" he asked. "Before you're ready to talk again."

"I don't know." She fished her keys out of her handbag as they climbed her front steps. The two-bedroom bungalow, painted light blue, seemed lonely and dark.

"I need some kind of timeline, Melissa. Come on. This isn't fair."

She acknowledged that he was right. Opening the door, she reached inside to flip on the porch light. It bathed them in a pale-yellow glow. She turned around in the doorway to face him. "How about a week."

"So we'll talk next Wednesday?"

"Yes."

"And this weekend? We're still on for Sunday dinner with your dad and Anita? We're still going to Whitney's dance performance on Friday?"

The possibility of canceling their plans surprised her. She'd been behaving as if everything were perfectly ordinary for so long now. Going through the motions. She'd gotten used to it.

"You don't want to?" she asked.

"It'll be awkward, that's all. Especially around your family."

But we're so good at pretending nothing's wrong, she thought. We've had plenty of practice since July. How many times have we seen Dad and Anita and acted as though we were still the same platonic pair as always?

He shook his head. "Never mind. I'll deal with it. We'll touch base tomorrow night, okay?"

She nodded.

"Melissa?"

"Yes?"

He raised a hand to her hair. She tried to hide a shiver as he stroked his fingers through the strands, rustling them and making her scalp tingle.

Why are you touching me like this? It isn't allowed. It's against the rules. I can't let you do this.

But it felt so good.

Kyle stopped and cupped the side of her face. "Don't worry. We'll work this out."

He turned around and left.

CHAPTER THREE

ONLY MELISSA.

Only Melissa, Kyle thought, could have kept her pregnancy secret for so damn long. Only she could have maintained the fiction that nothing had changed, could have managed not to reveal anything through words or expressions or actions. It was simply a logical extension of her business-as-usual performance after they'd made love.

Oh, Mel.

The woman was purely herself. She didn't try to act like anyone else.

He knew some people considered her inhuman, even cold. She wasn't. She might be more subtle, less immediately accessible. But the depth and the feelings were there. Only people who had no patience for subtlety had a hard time with her. People who needed everything to be simple and easy and obvious.

Kyle changed into sweats and shoved on his court shoes. It was Thursday afternoon and he'd made plans to meet his friend Jerome down at the park for some hoops. He needed the physical activity and the diversion of athletic competition. Badly.

His keys sat on his dresser, next to a framed photo of Felicity and him. He grabbed the keys and stuffed them into the zippered pocket of his sweatpants, then jogged down the stairs and left the building at an easy run, warming up his body slowly. The October air felt cool and refreshing against his skin. The change to standard time hadn't occurred yet, so a few more hours of daylight remained this afternoon.

He tilted up his face to the sun, briefly closing his eyes as he ran along the sidewalk, and thought, *How could this have happened? This impossible, incomprehensible situation. How can Melissa and I be having a baby together?*

Neither of them had expected to have children— let alone with each other.

How strange and terrifying...

Not that either of them had something against kids. No, they both liked them. They'd enjoyed the times when Kyle's brother and his wife—now his ex-wife—had come to visit, bringing little Danny and Mira. They often volunteered to baby-sit for friends.

But to take on parenthood themselves?

Kyle reached the park, saw Jerome and waved as he jogged toward him.

"Hey," the other man said, clasping his hand in

a quick man-to-man shake when he reached the court. "How's it going, Kyle?"

He shrugged. "You know."

I'm going to be a father.

The thought resounded in his head like the echoing announcements in a sports arena. He tried to ignore it and said, "Ready to be the old farts who kick some seventeen-year-old butts?"

Jerome laughed. "You bet, man."

Within a couple minutes they'd found more players and started a game. Kyle worked up a sweat. As the only white guy this afternoon—and one who was only five-eleven at that—he had to work extra hard to prove himself. And then there was the age thing. He and Jerome were thirty-two and thirty-six respectively. The teenagers here really did see them as old farts.

I'm going to be a father.

He jumped up and aimed for the hoop. The ball made a satisfying *whoosh* as it slid cleanly through; unlike some public courts, this one had nets hanging.

Jerome tagged him on the arm as they moved back out. "Good shot, buddy."

"Thanks."

I'm going to be a father. They played another thirty minutes before taking a break. Kyle walked over to the water fountain, breathing hard. He wiped the sweat from his forehead with the back of his forearm.

A few yards away children laughed and shouted as they pumped back and forth on the swings and climbed all over the brightly painted jungle gym.

Hell.

I'm going to be a father.

Jerome caught up with him as he leaned down for a drink. "Hey, old man," he teased. "Too much for you?"

Kyle swallowed a mouthful of water. "I'm not the one who was gasping and wheezing on the court back there," he said, and took another long gulp.

His friend laughed.

Kyle felt dizzy and weak. And it wasn't because of the basketball game.

ANITA LOPEZ did not look forward to seeing her sister. She loved Melissa and usually enjoyed spending time together—but sometimes the tensions in their relationship were more than she wanted to deal with.

And sometimes her perfect, overachieving sister could be a royal pain.

This Friday morning, Anita feared, was going to be one of those times. Especially after she told her the news. Without a doubt Melissa would flip.

Oh, she wouldn't shout and wave her arms in the air, or swear, or do any of the things *most* people did when they flew off the handle. No, Melissa would stay completely calm. Her very noticeable *lack* of a strong response would signal her flipped-outedness.

Through the kitchen window of her ground-floor apartment Anita saw her sister's white Honda pull up in the parking lot.

She'd been washing dishes from breakfast. She rinsed the last plate and wiped off her hands.

Melissa had almost reached the front stoop when Anita opened the door. They greeted each other with the genuine affection they shared—despite the issues between them—and Anita ushered her inside.

"I made some herbal tea to take with us," Anita said, "since I noticed you stopped drinking coffee last month."

"Thanks, that sounds great."

"Just let me get a wool sweater. It's a bit nippy out today, isn't it?"

When she returned from the bedroom, Melissa had retrieved the two insulated travel mugs from the kitchen counter. She handed one to Anita. "What's Troy up to this morning?"

"Working for his brother at the hardware store. Didn't I tell you?" She grabbed her backpack and keys from the dining-room table and they headed outside. "He started working there to pick up some extra cash."

"Mmm. I don't remember hearing about it."

They passed Melissa's car. They were going to shop at a little commercial area a mile or so away, and Melissa had suggested walking in order to get some exercise.

Anita shrugged as they reached the street and started off down the sidewalk. "I probably forgot to mention it. I've been...distracted lately."

"Painting a lot?"

"No, it's just..." She swallowed. How did you tell your younger sister, who'd never made a mistake in her life, that you'd gotten yourself knocked up? "Anyway, um, Troy had to leave before you got here. He said to say hello and he'll see you on Sunday at Dad's."

Melissa glanced at her. "He's going to be there?"

So far Troy hadn't made a lot of appearances at the Lopez family dinners. Their old-fashioned father hadn't quite accepted the man who was living in sin with her. She and Troy had decided to take it slowly instead of forcing the matter.

But now everything had changed.

"Melissa," she began, "Troy and I have some news..." Damn it. Her voice sounded high-pitched and shaky, but she had to go on. "That's why he's coming to dinner on Sunday—so we can tell Dad together."

"What kind of news? Do you mind telling me now or did you want to wait?"

"No, I don't want to wait."

Melissa watched her for a moment as they walked along the busy street. "So...?"

"So, it's just that—well—I know you're not going to like this," she blurted, "but I'm—I'm going to have a baby."

Silence met her announcement. She was afraid to meet her sister's gaze, which was silly.

Anita flipped up the spout on her travel mug and took a long gulp of tea. She kept waiting for Melissa to say something in that composed, even voice of hers but the silence continued, stretching out between them. They crossed an intersection and walked half a block.

Finally she risked a glance.

Good Lord, she thought. Her sister's face had gone pale. All the blood had drained out, giving her a deathly look. She was really upset. It was even worse than Anita had expected.

"Mel?" Anita asked.

Her sister cleared her throat. "Um, this is a surprise," she said. Her voice sounded funny.

"I know, but it just happened."

"It...wasn't a planned pregnancy, you mean?"

"No, it wasn't." Anita heard the defensive edge in her voice, but she couldn't help it. Cripes. She wished this didn't have to be such a huge, awful, upsetting thing. She wanted it to be no big deal—if not a wonderful, joyous, exciting thing...

"And Troy is the father?" Melissa asked.

She crossed her arms. "Of course he is. I'm only a few weeks pregnant."

"I'm sorry," Melissa said. "I didn't mean to insult you. I just wanted to be sure I understood."

"Well, you can be sure." She sounded petulant. Stupid to let herself get like this, she thought. Hadn't she wanted to convince Melissa she could be a mature adult? "Look," she said, sighing, "I didn't mean to say it like that. But I'm positive Troy's the father. I haven't been with anyone else since early spring."

"I see." Melissa stared down at her insulated mug, still sealed shut. "How does he feel about it?"

"Very good, actually. He's happy. So am I, for that matter." *And I wish you were, too,* she thought. *Jeez, Melissa, why can't you just be happy for me?*

"What are your plans?" Melissa asked.

"Well, I'm not having an abortion, if that's what you're asking."

"Are the two of you going to get married?"

"I don't know. Maybe, but later. I don't want to have a hasty wedding just because I'm pregnant."

Melissa didn't reply. She took a sip of tea, her movements a bit too precise as she opened the spout and raised it to her lips. "Mmm," she said. "This is good."

"Thanks. It's my own recipe. Helps with the morning sickness."

"You—have morning sickness?"

"Yes. Doesn't everyone? At least the first trimester, I mean?"

Melissa paused, her expression unreadable. "Actually, no."

"Oh." Anita shrugged. "Well, I'm one of the lucky ones, I guess."

"They say it helps to eat several small meals. And to take your time getting out of bed in the morning."

"Okay, I'll try that. Someone also suggested those wrist bands for motion sickness."

"I've heard that, too."

Why on earth, Anita thought, were they talking about something as unimportant as morning sickness right now? Especially when Melissa still looked as if she'd been attacked by a bloodsucking vampire.

How inane.

"You know," Melissa said, "if you and Troy got married, that might be the best thing for the baby."

And it would certainly be easier on Dad.

Of course she didn't say it, but Anita heard the unspoken message. Though he didn't attend church every Sunday, their father was still very Catholic. His beliefs remained traditional. It had been bad enough when Anita announced she was moving in with her boyfriend. For her to have a baby out of wedlock...

She inhaled deeply. "Look, I know it's going to

be hard for everyone to adjust to this. But I'm not ready to get married. In the long run I think it will be better for everyone, including the baby, if its parents don't rush into a premature commitment.''

She braced herself to hear Melissa's excruciatingly logical, well-measured, intelligent concerns. To hear her point out how poorly timed—how very *premature*—this pregnancy was. And, after all, if she and Troy were going to keep the child, to accept this sudden change in their lives and raise their son or daughter together, then why not go ahead and marry?

Anita knew she couldn't explain why she felt the way she did. She wasn't even sure she *wouldn't* be ready to marry Troy before the baby came. She just knew she didn't want to do it right now.

And she wasn't going to do it just because society said she should.

Surprisingly, though, Melissa didn't say a thing. Her face was still bloodless and pinched—attesting to her ongoing freak-out—but she made no attempts to reason with her.

Anita frowned. She'd also expected Melissa to ask how she'd gotten pregnant in the first place.

She'd dreaded that moment, dreaded the censure she would see in her sister's eyes, because she and Troy hadn't used contraception that night.

They'd been careless. They'd run out of condoms and forgotten to buy a new box, and they'd foolishly decided to take the risk.

But Melissa didn't ask about that, either. She seemed, in fact, to have shifted to a different plane of reality. Her eyes had a glazed quality Anita had never seen before and she walked like an automaton.

"Jeez," Anita said. "Are you okay?"

Melissa blinked and slowly focused on her.

"Hello? Is my sister in there?"

"I'm fine. Sorry, Anita. I'm just…I'm just…"

"You don't seem fine."

"No, probably not," Melissa murmured. "All right, it isn't true. I'm *not* fine. It's just so complicated."

"I know it is. But you have to trust me to work it all out—on my own. I can handle it, Sis. Please believe me."

"You don't understand." Melissa shook her head. She stared straight ahead and when they reached another intersection she groped for the crosswalk button without looking at it.

"What is it that I don't understand?"

"It's not just because you're pregnant. It's more than that. Oh, Anita. I'm pregnant, too."

CHAPTER FOUR

KYLE WALKED OVER to Melissa's house shortly after six. They were supposed to go out for dinner before heading to Whitney's dance performance.

Friday night and it looked like a date—why hadn't he and Melissa ever acknowledged how much they acted like a couple?

Because we had such a platonic friendship, he thought.

The boundaries had seemed so clear. But now everything had gotten blurry. Like when he took out his contacts and he couldn't find the edges of things.

Melissa wasn't just his best friend anymore. She was the woman with whom he was having a baby. For the rest of their lives they would have that between them. They would always be the parents of the son or daughter they'd created together.

Their child.

Kyle hadn't seen Melissa since Wednesday. He didn't know what to expect tonight. More business as usual? Or had they finally crossed the line?

Kyle climbed her front steps and knocked on the

door. His pulse, he realized, had accelerated sharply. Damn. He was nervous. Like a teenager.

Melissa didn't open the door. Nothing happened at all, in fact. Belatedly he noticed the house was dark, no lights shining out into the deepening dusk.

He stood on the porch about twenty seconds, oddly inert, not knowing what to do. Where the heck was she? He couldn't believe she would blow him off.

Finally he tried the door handle. It turned. He pushed the door inward, calling out as he stepped inside. No answer.

He switched on the light in the entryway. Melissa's handbag lay on the sideboard where she always tossed it when she got home. He stared at it. If she'd gone out she would have taken her handbag.

Fear unfurled inside him. "Melissa? You home?" Snapping to life, he rounded the corner to the living room with urgent steps. Someone could have broken in. Attacked her—

He lurched to a sudden halt. She sat on the couch in the darkened room, her spine straight, her hands folded neatly on her lap. "Melissa? Oh, God. Are you okay?"

In the light from the entryway he saw her blink. Her eyes seemed focused on the opposite wall. She didn't make a sound, but a moment later she gave a small nod.

Once again Kyle couldn't move. Relief hit his

system like a chemical substance, overwhelming and intense.

He found his voice. "Jesus, Melissa, you scared the shit out of me. I thought you'd—I thought someone had—"

She still didn't look at him. He took a few steps toward her. Silence filled the room and in that silence he became aware of the fast, shallow sound of her breath.

A moment later her body crumpled on the couch.

MELISSA WAS DIMLY AWARE of Kyle pulling her onto his lap. When had he sat down next to her? He stroked her hair back from her face and held her torso against his chest, rocking her.

Her fingers tingled. Some of them had gone numb. She tried to slow her breathing. She took deep, shuddering gulps of air.

"That's right," he soothed. "It's okay."

God, this was the kind of thing Anita would do. Or a patient. Not her. She was the doctor, who treated others. She wasn't supposed to be the one with a problem.

Melissa gasped again, and suddenly she was crying. She sobbed against Kyle's neck, her tears running down to dampen his collar. Her body shook violently, unattractively, and he hugged her close.

"It's okay, Mel. I'm here for you."

All the stress of the past few months worked its

way to the surface. She couldn't hide it anymore, couldn't keep pushing it down.

Gradually her breathing evened out as she gave in to it. She hadn't cried like this in a very long time. Even on the gut-wrenching night when they'd ended up making love...

"Oh, God," she mumbled.

He pulled a tissue from the box on the end table and handed it to her.

She paused long enough to blow her nose, then more sobs overtook her.

Finally, a few minutes later, her body slowly stilled. She felt a sense of calm seep into her limbs. She accepted another tissue and blotted her face, her swollen eyes. "I'm sorry," she said.

"Don't be." He held her against him, against his broad, solid chest.

Melissa realized she still sat on his lap. Curled up like a child. She shifted self-consciously, unused to being in such a vulnerable position. Not even *as* a child had she been held like this—at least, not since the accident. Her father had been too overcome with grief and despair, too busy resisting the urge to die, to have the energy. And Anita had been too distraught, as well. She'd needed *Melissa* to provide the comforting gestures their father couldn't.

"What a mess I am," she said.

Kyle didn't release her. "Shhh. It doesn't matter.'' He kissed her forehead. ''Tell me what happened.''

She swallowed. ''I'm pregnant,'' she said with a feeble little laugh.

''What else?''

''Maybe it's hormonal.''

''Maybe,'' he said. ''What else happened?''

She inhaled deeply, let the air out in a sigh. Had she ever appreciated the simple ability to breathe before? Not like this. ''Oh, Kyle. It's my sister.''

''You told her about the baby?''

She nodded. ''It's crazy. She… I'm not the only one who's pregnant.''

A few seconds passed. Kyle reached over and switched on a reading lamp. He cradled her against his other shoulder and they blinked at each other as their eyes adjusted.

He frowned in disbelief. ''Are you serious? You mean—?''

''She's due in June. I wasn't going to tell her about my pregnancy, but then she told me about hers.''

''It knocked you off balance.'' He traced the curve of her face.

''Way off. I couldn't believe it.'' Melissa closed her eyes. ''Why now?''

''You're worried about your father.''

''Of course. He'll probably have a heart attack. The worst thing is, Anita doesn't want to get married. She and Troy are staying together, but she says she's not ready for anything more. That means he'll have two unmarried, pregnant daughters at the same time.''

''You really think it'll be too much for him?''

Melissa met his gaze again. ''I love my dad, Kyle. But he's fragile. When my mom and brother died...he fell apart.''

''Well, who wouldn't? This isn't quite the same thing, though.''

''I know, but it will still be a shock. He's so old-fashioned.'' She scooted off Kyle's lap and stood. ''I need to wash my face, okay?''

He followed her to the bathroom and leaned a shoulder against the door frame while she splashed water on her face. Her features were puffy, but the cold water helped. She patted her face with a soft white hand towel.

''I feel better,'' she told him, straightening the towel on the rack. ''Thank you for taking care of me. For being there.''

''Of course, Mel, we're friends.'' He took a step into the room and pulled her into his arms before she even had a thought of stopping him. He kissed her forehead again and moved his lips to her temple, inhaling. ''Mmm.''

It happened so quickly. One moment she was recovering from an emotional episode, the next moment an acute physical awareness filled her whole body. Melissa started to pull away, but when she did his lips traced a path from her temple to her mouth. And they were kissing.

They hadn't kissed since July. Now that seemed like only yesterday. This felt so natural, so easy.

So automatic.

The kiss wasn't outrageous. No tongues, no frantic moans or angling of heads. Just a simple, hot meeting of lips. Spellbinding. Gentle and soft and sexy. Like a kiss between a longtime couple, familiar and intimate.

And then Kyle ended it and rested his forehead against hers. They both breathed more quickly now, but this time it was arousal.

"That didn't feel like friends," she managed to say.

"I know. I'm sorry." He didn't sound particularly regretful. His voice had a ragged quality. "Want to pretend it didn't happen?"

"Oh, yes. Definitely."

She stepped out of his arms. They walked to the kitchen and it was as if the interlude had never happened.

Her body still humming, she opened the refrigerator door. "Let's skip the restaurant tonight, okay? I have some leftovers we can graze on."

He nodded and they pulled out some food. They were acting like an old married couple in the kitchen.

Kyle poured them glasses of water and sat down

at the kitchen table. "You still up for Whitney's dance thing?"

She joined him with a collection of utensils and a couple more containers of food. "Actually, yes. I think it will be good for me. Would you mind driving, though?"

"Not at all."

They ate in silence for a minute.

She said, "I know I told you I didn't want to talk until Wednesday." About their situation. The baby they had conceived. "But Anita's pregnancy changes things. She and Troy plan to tell Dad at dinner on Sunday. I think we should, too. It wouldn't be right to listen to their announcement and not make our own."

"Are you sure?"

She shrugged and took a bite of pasta salad.

"Don't you think they'll have a lot of questions?" Kyle said. "About you and me, that is."

"I already told Anita." She watched his expression change. He looked almost tense. Normally he was so easygoing, she thought, so unconcerned. *She* was supposed to be the uptight one.

"Told her what exactly?"

"I told her we'd gotten together one night."

He swallowed a bite of rotisserie chicken. "Oh? What did she say?"

"She was shocked. She asked if *we* were getting married. I said no, of course."

"Mmm. So, what do you want to tell your dad?"

"That's the thing. I don't know. Maybe I should say I don't know who the father is."

"Right." He shook his head. "I don't think so."

"I could say it's someone I met at a medical conference. Someone from, say, Cleveland."

"Any particular reason?"

She shrugged again.

"Melissa, it's not going to work. We have to tell him I'm the father."

"He'll be mad at you. Madder than he'll be at Troy, I'm sure." At least Troy and Anita shared a household; at least they were a real couple.

"Fine. I'll take the heat. I'd rather do that than hide behind an imaginary guy from Cleveland."

"God…maybe we *should* get married. It would make this so much easier."

"I'm sorry?"

She shook her head. "I don't know. It was just an idea."

"A crazy one," he said.

"Can you come up with something better?"

Kyle thought for a moment. "Maybe not. You're sure we should tell him on Sunday?"

"Yes. I've already told Anita. She doesn't want to have to keep the secret. Anyway, she's afraid she'd accidentally spill the beans."

"But finding out about you and Anita at once—"

"Will be even harder on Dad. A double whammy. Yes, I know." She paused. Reached across the table for a gingersnap. "If we could tell him we were getting *married*, though…"

Kyle set down his silverware. He leaned forward and captured her gaze. "You keep saying that and I don't know why. You're not serious."

He was right, Melissa thought. She couldn't be serious. It was too outrageous. Too extreme.

And she didn't miss the flicker of panic in his eyes. Marriage and Kyle? No, not since Felicity had that been a possibility, and it wouldn't be for years to come.

Not too difficult to figure out that the suicide of a loved one was even harder to get over than a regular death. Not too difficult to figure out why Kyle kept his love life shallow and uncommitted.

And her own feelings about marriage? The subject was an uncomfortable one. She didn't like to go there. She hadn't expected it to be an issue. The two proposals she'd received in her life had not even remotely tempted her. She found it impossible to imagine herself as a wife, as part of a happy little picket-fence family.

But this wasn't a normal situation, she thought. It felt unreal, as if they'd slipped into an alternative universe.

One in which marriage might be a strangely appropriate solution.

"Mel," he persisted, "tell me you're not serious."

"I don't know, Kyle. What if I were? What if we could have an old-fashioned marriage of convenience?"

"What in God's name is that?"

"One that's not based on romance. One based on other things. Like—"

"Convenience. Come on, Mel. That's crazy."

"Is it, though?" She frowned, trying to think it through. "We get along well. We want the same things in life. Oh, Kyle. Marriage could be the smartest way to handle our circumstances."

"What you're talking about is a shotgun wedding. The thing your sister refuses to have."

"Fine," Melissa said. "I'm not my sister, though."

THEY DISCUSSED IT on the way to the dance performance. Kyle thought she'd lost her mind. And maybe she had. Maybe she'd damaged her brain cells when she'd hyperventilated. A week ago she would never have considered such a radical solution.

But she felt very calm. And very sane. And the more they talked about it the surer she became. Why *not* get married? Neither of them had looked forward to a regular marriage someday; this wouldn't get in the way of a future relationship.

She realized, too, that matrimony seemed so

much safer without the complication of romantic love. So much less disturbing.

The idea of having a child already disturbed her enough—more than she could ever acknowledge out loud. It scared her. The fear wasn't rational. It was deep and instinctual. Sometimes she thought she'd simply seen too much at work and in her own family not to be aware of the risks of losing people. Of the potential for devastating pain. Despair that took away your ability to get through the day. Your will to live.

How many times had she had to tell people their child or spouse had died? Enough to know she didn't want to be on the other end of that conversation.

And it never got any easier. Sometimes it even got harder—when one of her patients somehow got under her skin. Like last July.

And now, because of that day, she would be a parent after all. She would accept the risks because abortion and adoption were even less acceptable to her. And she might marry Kyle, too—if she could talk him into it.

"All right," Kyle finally said. "Let's sleep on it. Maybe you'll come to your senses by morning."

"Maybe not," she said.

A minute later he pulled up outside their destination, a small, avant-garde theater in southeast Portland, and cut the engine. "This place is creepy looking," he said, grinning. "Like it might not be good for a pregnant lady."

"Oh, please. Don't start coddling me." She didn't want him to treat her any differently because of her breakdown tonight. It had only been temporary. She was still a strong person. She didn't need to be sheltered from every little thing.

"Right," he said, and exited his blue Toyota.

But he circled the vehicle and helped her out. And all the way into the theater his hand rested between her shoulder blades. It could have been a simple, friendly, gentlemanly gesture. But it felt like more. It felt both protective and possessive.

They ran into Barbara Purcell in the lobby.

She stared at them for a long moment. "You two okay?"

"Sure," Kyle said. "Why wouldn't we be?"

"Something's going on. Want to let me in on it?"

Melissa forced a smile. *Oh, Barbara. You'd be stunned if we did. I'm still stunned.* "It's no big deal. We'll tell you about it later, okay?"

As soon as we figure out what to do. What to say. Whether we're going to be husband and wife.

And we've got to make the decision soon. Before we talk to my father on Sunday.

Kyle placed that possessive hand on her back again as the three of them went to find their seats. She was pretty sure Barbara noticed, though the other woman made no comment.

WHAT WAS WRONG WITH HIM? He couldn't keep his hands off her, Kyle reflected as he pulled out of the theater parking lot after the performance. He told himself to cool it. He didn't *want* them to do anything physical again. Yet tonight his body had ignored his brain's commands. He'd even kissed her.

Beside him Melissa stared thoughtfully out the window.

"What are you thinking about?" he asked, wanting distraction from his own ruminations.

"Barbara. I didn't realize we were so obvious. No one noticed anything before."

"Last summer, you mean." No one had noticed anything different between them after they'd made love.

She nodded.

So now they were no longer able to act normal together—the way they had for months.

They were having a baby. Unlike the single night they'd shared, this wasn't a discrete event that could ever be finished, ever be ignored. The shape of Melissa's body would soon reveal what was going on inside her. In the spring she would give birth. And their child would remain in their lives.

The knowledge had to affect their behavior. If Barbara had perceived a change, others might, too.

"Maybe my eyes were red," she said. "Maybe

that's what caught Barbara's attention. She could tell I'd been crying.''

"I don't think so," Kyle said. "Your eyes looked fine... You still think we should get hitched?''

She nodded. "You?''

"Nothing's changed in the past hour or two. I still can't see it.''

"Not to mention you're a confirmed bachelor.''

"Not to mention that.''

He couldn't believe Melissa had come up with the idea. She'd always been even more terrified of marriage and having a family than he was.

Even more self-protective.

And he didn't blame her. Who *wouldn't* be after what she'd gone through? The accident, losing her mother and brother, surviving when they hadn't. And afterward her father's grief, his longing to kill himself. Kyle didn't know how Melissa had found out about it—he hadn't had the heart to ask—but he'd often thought about what that knowledge would do to a kid.

His own experience with suicide made it easy for him to imagine.

And now Melissa worked in an E.R. Not a place to let her forget about human tragedy—or make her give up her emotional defenses.

Kyle frowned as he stared at the road in front of them. Perhaps her idea wasn't so surprising after all, he told himself.

A marriage of convenience, she'd called it. Not a regular one. A much less messy kind of partnership. No unruly emotions, no romantic love to complicate the arrangement.

Oh, Mel. Only you.

CHAPTER FIVE

ON SATURDAYS Kyle usually spent a couple of hours at the clinic. He arrived a bit later than planned, having overslept and then losing a good thirty minutes at the breakfast table, staring off into space. Barely touching his food. Thinking about marriage.

If nothing else it would please his mother. Like many parents she wanted her children to settle down—something neither of her sons had done with much success.

And six years had passed since Felicity. He knew his mother thought it was time to try again.

She adored Melissa, whom she'd met on her yearly trips to Portland, though she'd long since stopped dropping hints about their relationship. If Kyle and Melissa got married his mother would be overjoyed. Not a reason to do it, of course, but it was another factor to consider. He wouldn't mind giving his mother something to be happy about. She'd suffered enough in her life.

Kyle parked his car around the corner and walked to the clinic, greeting a few of the people he met on the sidewalk. This area of Portland, called Old Town, had a lot of residents—both the indoor and outdoor variety. After working here six years Kyle recognized most of them, and was friendly with many of them.

He wanted to do his part to help make the community a safer, healthier, more hopeful place. Slowly that seemed to be happening, but a lot of work remained to be done. And Old Town would never be the kind of carefree, complacent neighborhood like the ones in the west hills. Too much poverty here, for one thing.

But you couldn't let it get to you. Not too much. That was a sure way to burn out. Then you were no good to anyone.

Reaching the clinic, he pushed the door and stepped inside. Barbara had arrived a couple of hours earlier and opened up shop with the blond lawyer who volunteered most weekends. Kyle nodded at her and glanced around the waiting area, where a few people already sat.

His gaze landed on Zita, who'd already had an appointment a few days ago. He raised an eyebrow. "How's it going?"

She gave him a sour look. "Yeah, whatever. Trouble with my foot."

Her high-top sneakers had several large holes in them, affording him a glimpse of a dirty bandage on one heel.

"I'm sorry to hear that," he said. "I'm sure Barbara will help you take care of that."

"Where's Doc Lopez?"

For some reason she'd taken a shine to Melissa, even though she ended up yelling at her more often than not during her regular checkups for hypertension and a few other conditions.

"Sorry. She only works Wednesdays."

"Damn it! Oh, well, Barbara's cool, too. It's that other one—" She snapped her fingers in front of her forehead a couple of times.

"Dr. Griffin?"

"Yeah, him. He's a pig."

Ross Griffin was a very nice young resident who worked with Melissa up at Northwest Hospital and volunteered whenever his schedule allowed. He was hardly "a pig," but Kyle refrained from pointing that out. He wouldn't be able to change her mind.

"Lucky for you he's not in today," he said, turning to go to his office. "See you around, Zita. I hope your foot gets better."

"Sure, fine. Whatever."

He smiled as he let himself into his office. Coming from Zita that was pretty polite.

He made slow but steady progress on his paperwork, despite his preoccupied state. At one point Barbara dropped in and shared a cup of coffee. She watched him a little more closely than usual, he thought, but she didn't refer to the previous night.

A little before noon he glanced up from his desk to see a boy, maybe sixteen, standing in the doorway to his office. His light-brown hair hung in greasy tangles around his face and his clothes looked as if they hadn't seen a washing machine in months. His left wrist was in a splint. He carried an army-surplus duffel bag over his shoulder.

Street kid. He didn't appear drugged out, Kyle noted—good sign for his future health and safety.

"That black lady said you had some stuff you could give me." His voice was only slightly sullen.

Kyle stood. "Okay. Personal supplies, that kind of thing?" he asked, walking to the wall shelves.

The boy shrugged, staring down at the peeling linoleum floor. "Yeah, I guess so," he muttered.

Kyle pulled out a couple of cardboard boxes. "Why don't you come see what you can use."

The kid hesitated.

"My name's Kyle. What's yours?"

More hesitation. Then, "Blue."

A street name. Not surprising that he wouldn't trust Kyle, a stranger, with his real name.

"Nice to meet you, Blue." He held up a packet with a toothbrush, toothpaste, deodorant and soap. "This look like stuff you need?"

Blue took a few steps into the room. "It's free, right?"

Kyle nodded.

"Yeah, okay. I guess I could use that." He walked over and accepted the packet.

Kyle saw his gaze dart to the contents of the

second box. "Anything else you're interested in? Sometimes the good stuff gets hidden in the bottom. Feel free to dig around."

The kid did so after a little more prompting, selecting a roll of antacids and several other items. He stuffed them all into his duffel bag, glancing around as if he were shoplifting and expected a security guard to walk up any second.

Kyle put the boxes back onto the shelves. "You know about Buddy's Café?"

Blue shook his head. "Never heard of it."

"Well, it's a good place to get a meal."

"It's not like a…soup kitchen, is it? I don't go to those. The food always sucks and all they care about is getting you to read the Bible."

Not strictly true, Kyle thought, but he didn't argue. "No, it's not a soup kitchen."

He gave Blue a brief description of Buddy's. Located a couple of blocks away, the nonprofit restaurant served good-tasting, well-balanced meals for a nominal charge. If you couldn't pay for your food you could work for it, doing dishes, taking out the trash, bussing tables and so on.

"You should check it out," Kyle said.

"Maybe." The kid's tone was noncommittal, but Kyle detected a veiled interest in his eyes.

He walked over to his desk for a card with the clinic's hours printed on it. "I'm going to write down the café's address in case you want to try it.

Also a couple of other places that might interest you.''

A shelter for teens. Some advocacy resources. That was about all he could do.

Blue glanced down at the card a little cynically. This wasn't the first time someone had tried to help him. ''Yeah, okay. Thanks for the stuff.''

''If there's anything else I can do for you don't hesitate to let me know. I mean that.''

''Sure. Uh, thanks again.''

Blue slunk out of the office. Kyle wondered if he would ever see him a second time.

Maybe Blue would return to his parents. But sometimes the homes these kids had left really *were* worse than a life on the streets.

Kyle made a mental note to ask around the staff at Buddy's next time he was there. See if Blue had paid a visit.

Shortly afterward he packed up and left.

BACK AT HOME Kyle spent the afternoon in a deeply restless state. He played basketball with Jerome, cleaned his car, repaired his broken toaster oven, even baked an apple pie.

Marriage on his mind all along.

His brother, Craig, called while the pie was cooling on the counter.

''Hey, Kyle. It's been a few weeks since we've talked. What's new?''

"Not much."

Kyle hated to lie by omission, but he couldn't mention Melissa's pregnancy yet. If Craig had called in a day or two the situation might have changed, but for now Kyle had to talk around it. He sat at the dining table with his cordless phone and described the health clinic's fund-raising progress.

"How about you?" he asked a few minutes later. "Any big cases lately?"

Craig was a lawyer in Boston, where they'd grown up. Ever since his divorce last year he'd been especially devoted to his work. He told Kyle about a couple of the cases he was handling.

"And how are my niece and nephew?" Kyle asked.

"Pretty good, I guess. Mira's learning the alphabet at preschool and Danny has a new pet mouse—named Mousey."

Kyle laughed. "You still get to see them every Sunday?"

"Yeah." Craig sounded unhappy. "It's not the same as living with them, though. One day a week together when you used to have seven? It stinks."

"I bet it does." He got up to water the ficus. "Damn, I'm sorry you don't have custody."

"Me, too. But I knew it would become ugly if I pushed. Didn't want to put Danny and Mira through that."

Kyle filled a watering can with tap water and took it to the plant. "Think you'll ever try to re-open the case?"

"Probably. In a year or two when their mother's tired of using them to get to me."

"You'll be able to stand it that long?"

"Don't have a choice. I sure do miss my kids, though. And I still feel guilty Sarah and I couldn't work things out. I didn't want them to have to grow up in a broken family. Especially after what happened when we were little. I wanted them to have two parents at home."

They talked a couple more minutes before hanging up. Kyle sat at the table again, motionless.

Synchronicity.

He'd expected Craig's call this weekend and their conversation had been a typical one; none of the topics was new. But now his brother's concerns about Danny and Mira struck a little too close to home.

If he and Melissa didn't marry, Kyle wouldn't live with his own son or daughter. In effect, his situation would be the same as Craig's. True, Melissa would let him see the baby more than once a week. But he knew his brother was right.

It wouldn't be the same.

God, was he really considering marriage? Despite everything?

While growing up, he'd watched his mother

struggle as a lonely, heartbroken single parent. He'd been wounded himself by his father's abandonment and promised himself not to be like the selfish, uncaring man who'd deserted their family, never to be heard from again. But he'd recognized parts of his father in himself anyway. Secretly he'd wondered if he wasn't cut from the same cloth.

Then he'd met Felicity. Fallen in love with her and convinced himself everything would work out. Summoned the courage to ask her to marry him.

He supposed it had helped, in a way, that she couldn't have children. He'd known he would never have to face that test.

They'd started to plan a wedding and a life together. But that hadn't been enough to make her pain and despair go away—pain and despair he hadn't fully realized existed. He'd often wondered why she'd bothered to accept his proposal. Or whether planning a life with him had been what had pushed her over the edge.

He hadn't seen the suicide coming. That was the worst part of it. The part that made him feel as inadequate as his father had been.

By the time Craig had gotten divorced Kyle had already figured it out: the people in his family weren't meant to have long-term relationships. No—they were always leaving or getting left. He wouldn't go down that road again. Wouldn't consider marriage again.

Yet Melissa's proposition made a crazy kind of sense. His circumstances had changed now. He was going to be a father. He didn't want to miss out on his son's or daughter's childhood if he could be a full-time dad.

A marriage of convenience would be the best way to ensure he had a solid presence in his kid's life.

Abruptly Kyle swung to his feet. He collected the pie and took it downstairs to his elderly neighbors, then continued outside for a long, soul-searching walk.

Sunday mornings were slow in the E.R., so Melissa was able to catch up on sleep after a typically hectic Saturday night. Around 11:00 a.m. she wandered down to the cafeteria in her scrubs.

She chose fruit salad and yogurt and oatmeal and juice, and faithfully took her prenatal vitamin pills. Soon, she thought, she would have to tell her boss about her pregnancy. She would probably work until her seventh or eighth month, but only on a reduced schedule. No more overnight shifts; just nine to five, like a regular working person. The idea had some appeal, she thought.

She still didn't have any nausea. Her skin felt a little more sensitive, the way it did right before her period, but that was the only seminegative symptom. She'd been getting her rest lately, mainly because the E.R. was inexplicably well staffed this fall. When she'd stepped on the scale a few days ago she'd been pleased to see she'd gained some weight.

So far so good with her pregnancy. Everything else, however…

The jury was still out.

Just as she was finishing breakfast Kyle appeared beside her table.

"They told me I could find you here," he said. "How are you doing?"

She stared up at him. Sunlight streamed in through a nearby window, illuminating his tanned skin. He wore jeans and a heather-gray T-shirt. Not that Melissa wanted to notice, but he looked particularly good today. A couple of medical students at the next table eyed him up and down appreciatively and actually giggled.

"I'm fine," she said.

"Not too bad a night at work?"

"No, just the usual. Saturday-night fistfights. No shootings. One drunken driving accident. I'm surprised to see you here."

"I know. Sorry I didn't page you before stopping by, but I was afraid you'd be asleep. Didn't want to take the chance of waking you up."

"Coddling me again?"

He smiled. "Mind if I grab a cup of coffee?"

"Sure. Then we can go to my office."

She returned her tray and waited for him near the exit, wondering what he would say this morning. Since Friday night she'd become more and more convinced that they should get married. And not just because of her father.

She wasn't afraid of being a single parent and she knew plenty of people who'd done a great job at it—but she also felt that two parents in the household were better than one. Together she and Kyle would be able to give their child the best life possible.

She hoped he had realized that, as well.

"I got you some peppermint tea," he said, joining her.

"Thanks."

Typical Kyle, she thought. Always considerate and attentive. *He would make a good father.*

As long as he was actually committed to the role…

She accepted the paper cup and they started off down the hallway.

"How are you feeling about what happened on Friday?" he asked.

"Okay. I guess I just needed to lose it. It's been so stressful lately. I feel a lot better now, though. And you were great that night. Thank you."

"No problem."

Even on a Sunday morning the hospital hummed with activity. A couple of people stopped Melissa to talk, so it was a few minutes before they reached her little office. She closed the door and joined Kyle on the couch where she took most of her naps, though there was another room to sleep in right off the E.R.

Kyle finished his coffee and set the cup down on a corner table. ''I've done a lot of thinking this weekend.''

''Yes, me, too,'' she said.

''You still willing to marry me?''

CHAPTER SIX

MELISSA WASN'T PREPARED for the sharp way her stomach dipped when he spoke the words. She felt as if the couch had dropped out from underneath her. As if he'd just made a regular proposal.

God, they were going to be husband and wife. Going to raise their child together.

"You're really sure about this?" she asked, needing to confirm the proposal was real.

Even though she was the one who'd dreamed up the idea, she felt stunned. Suddenly the whole course of her life had been altered. Again. So much turmoil and change in the past few months. Almost too much to comprehend.

"Yes, I'm sure." Kyle took the cup from her hand and set it down beside his. He turned to face her, reaching for her hands. His skin warmed hers, his touch giving her a sense of comfort and reassurance. "I needed a while," he said, "but I've realized it's the best choice for all of us. You and me, the baby, our families… So what do you say?"

For a moment she couldn't answer. She held his hazel-eyed gaze and the next twenty years flashed in her mind. Diaper changings and nighttime feedings. Bedtime stories. Puppet shows and ice-cream cones, school plays and picnics. Ball games, family vacations, college applications...

"Melissa?"

She cleared her throat. "Yes," she said, her voice husky. "Yes, let's get married."

They smiled at each other. He pulled her toward him for a gentle hug. They breathed a shared sigh of relief, as if they'd just survived a hurricane.

Melissa's pager went off, its buzzing abnormally loud in the quiet room.

"Oh, jeez." She pulled away and glanced at the digital display. "They need me back at the E.R. I'm sorry, Kyle."

He shrugged and stood up with her. "You're at work. I knew we'd be interrupted, but I didn't want to wait. We'll talk some more this afternoon, okay?"

Before they went to her father's house.

"Yes," she said, "we'd better. Come over around four?"

MELISSA WAS KNEELING in her vegetable garden, showered and dressed in jeans and a wool sweater and planting garlic for next summer's crop, when Kyle arrived. She'd left him a note on the front door and he'd circled the house to the backyard.

He wore a leather jacket over his T-shirt, and a gentle breeze ruffled his dark-brown hair. She watched him in the slanting afternoon light as he approached, and was overwhelmed by the realization that he was her fiancé now.

He crouched beside her. "You should have gotten me to do that," he said, meaning the garlic.

"Why?"

"Because I'll probably end up enjoying more of the harvest than you will." He set about helping her, adding a scoop of organic fertilizer to each of the planting holes. "Since you're doing this," he said mildly, "I take it you'd like to keep living here after we're married."

Melissa raised a gloved hand to her cheek, startled. "I didn't even think about that. I just wanted to get these in the ground before the next rainy spell."

"Hey, I'm happy to live here. Didn't you say the owner was thinking of selling? Maybe we could buy the place."

First they were having a child; now they might purchase a house together. "Next thing I know you'll want to buy a minivan," she said, teasing.

"God forbid." He reached over to brush her face with the pad of his thumb. "You got a smudge on your cheek."

They worked in silence for a moment. She thought of all the plans they would have to make. Arrangements for their new lives.

"I guess we're agreeing to stay together at least until our kid's in college," she said, grabbing a handful of garlic cloves and positioning one in each hole.

"I guess so." He considered her. "I *think* I can trust you not to run off with some gigolo before then."

She rolled her eyes. "Very funny… It's a long time, isn't it?"

"Yes."

"But I don't see any other way."

We've made our decision. Have to play it out. Because of the baby.

"No," he said, "me, neither…"

"Have you thought about what to say to our families?" she asked.

"Just that we're getting married. And then we can add that we're having a baby. That should come second."

She agreed. "I don't think we should mention the marriage-of-convenience part," she said. "It would be too confusing. Too complicated. Plus when the baby grows up, I don't want him or her to have to deal with it."

"No, me, neither. We can keep it between the two of us. But you know it's going to be hard at first."

Pretending to be a regular couple.

Yes, she thought. Initially they might feel uncomfortable, but they would get over it. No one except themselves should be burdened with the details of their arrangement.

They finished the planting and cleaned up, discussing the practical matters of the union. They agreed on a courthouse wedding and a small reception sometime during the next couple of weeks. Something mellow and quiet. Kyle would have to move in right afterward.

Into the spare bedroom.

After all, this was not a normal marriage.

Melissa had never shared a room with a man. She hadn't shared a room with *anyone* since she'd lived in a dorm in college. And sharing a bed was a whole other level of intimacy. Sleeping beside another person all night long, night after night...

Well, that wasn't what this marriage was about. And she wouldn't let herself think about it. Not yet. There were too many other matters to deal with first. She would put aside her concerns and ignore the shaky feeling in the pit of her stomach.

Inside the house she washed her hands and asked Kyle to meet her at his place in half an hour.

"I need to call Anita," she told him. "I want to give her some warning."

This was something else she felt nervous about. Somehow she had to tell her sister the news without hurting or upsetting her. Not an easy task.

Kyle left after a quick hug and a supportive pat on the shoulder. During the past week they'd shared more physical contact, she realized, than they usually did in a year.

Why didn't it bother her more?

She dialed Anita's number. Her sister picked up on the fourth ring, just as Melissa was mentally composing her message for the answering machine.

"Hi, Anita. It's Melissa."

"Oh, hey. Sorry, I was painting in the other room and had Elvis Costello cranked up too loud. What's up? You're still going to Dad's in an hour, aren't you?"

"Yes," Melissa assured her. "Kyle and I will be there." She paused. "You haven't changed your mind about that wedding, have you?"

"Sorry, Sis. I'm still not ready."

"Okay, then I need to ask you something..." She walked to the back window of the kitchen and stared out at the plot where she and Kyle had planted the garlic. It looked like a plain square of earth. Only in the spring would the top growth push up through the soil. "How would you feel if Kyle and I *did* have one?"

"Have one what?"

"A wedding."

"Oh." Anita sounded surprised. "Uh, fine, I guess. It's not really my business, though, is it?"

Melissa wasn't sure if her sister was being sarcastic or really meant it. "But it does affect you, since you're pregnant, too."

"How so?"

Melissa chose her words carefully. "Well, because of Dad's reaction to everything. If Kyle and

I get married, then he'll be a lot happier with us. Less disapproving of my pregnancy.''

''And more disapproving of Troy and me. We'll look worse in comparison. Is that what you mean?''

''Am I pissing you off? You sound kind of tense.''

Anita sighed. ''I'm sorry. I just wish you wouldn't worry about me so much.''

''Oh,'' she said, bewildered. ''I guess I was trying to be thoughtful.''

''I know you were, Melissa.'' Her sister's voice gentled. ''You were afraid I'd blame you. For being the good daughter, while I look like the bad one, having a baby out of wedlock.''

''Pretty much.'' Melissa poured herself a glass of orange juice and rested her hip against the counter, drinking it.

''I guess from my previous behavior that isn't very surprising. It's not as if I haven't gotten upset over things like that in the past. But I'm trying to grow up a little. I'm the one who's not ready for a wedding, so I'm the one who'll deal with Dad's reaction to it.''

Melissa pulled the phone from her ear and stared at it. What had *happened* to Anita lately? She realized she hadn't been paying close enough attention. She'd been operating on autopilot as far as their relationship was concerned, but her sister really had been changing. Especially since she and Troy had gotten their own apartment.

"Hey, are you there?"

Melissa returned the receiver to her ear. "Yes, sorry about that. I was just thinking."

"About what?"

"About how I need to stop trying to baby-sit you," she said, and meant it.

"Wellll…" Anita sounded amused. "That certainly wouldn't hurt."

They shared a chuckle. It felt good, Melissa decided. Sisterly.

"Hey, listen," Anita said. "About you and Kyle getting hitched. I'm a bit surprised—you seemed so definite about *not* doing it when we talked a few days ago."

Melissa took a deep breath, briefly wishing she could tell the whole story. But that wasn't possible. "I know, but we realized we care about each other. We've known each other a long time and it just feels right to us."

"Oh, okay. God, listen to me—now I'm being the worrywart. Well, for what it's worth, I'm really happy for you. I always hoped the two of you would end up together. Didn't think it would ever happen," she added, "but I'm definitely glad it did. So congratulations."

"Thank you," Melissa said, a bit confused.

Her sister had hoped she and Kyle would end up together?

But then, Anita had always been a romantic, despite her reluctance to marry right now. She saw couple potential everywhere she looked.

"Listen, I've got to clean up my paints. I'll see you at Dad's soon, okay?"

"Sure."

"And Melissa?"

"Mmm?"

"I love you."

TELLING HER FATHER wasn't quite as bad as Melissa had feared. But it wasn't pleasant. He was shocked and upset, especially with the men. Not that he wasn't disappointed in his daughters—but in his vision of society it was a man's fault for getting a girl in trouble.

All through the family dinner he repeatedly shook his head, as if in response to an unpleasant internal dialogue. His eyes did light up at the prospect of grandchildren, but they dimmed just as quickly when he couldn't convince Anita to marry in order to give her baby a name.

"He or she *will* have a name," she insisted. "Mine."

Ben Lopez stared across the table at Troy, disbelief in his aging features. "You're going to let her do this to your child?"

"I'm sorry, sir, but I don't exactly have a lot of choice." Troy, a pale, serious man with a goatee, attempted a smile. "I already proposed and she turned me down."

"I deferred my decision," Anita corrected. "I'm just not ready to do it right now."

The conversation moved on to Kyle, whom Ben felt had betrayed him and his daughter.

Shaking his head, he said, "I don't believe it. You were her friend. But if you'd respected her you would have married her first, not second."

"Oh, Dad," Melissa said. "It wasn't like that at all. And we're getting married soon, all right?"

"Soon," he repeated. "That makes it okay? You don't think people will be able to count back the months when you give birth?" Wearily he sighed. "Three months, almost. Your belly will get big before Christmas."

And that is too soon. Shamefully soon.

He didn't have to say the words.

Kyle, sitting beside her, set down his glass and put an arm around her shoulder. "I'm sorry about the way this happened, Mr. Lopez, but I care deeply about your daughter. I'm eager to marry her and have a family together."

The words had their intended effect. Mollified, Ben quizzed them about their plans for the future.

Melissa wondered, just for a moment, what it would be like if they were marrying for love. As they talked with her family, she could almost believe the illusion they'd created.

But neither of them wanted that kind of romantic

relationship. If not for her unexpected pregnancy Kyle probably would have remained a bachelor for a long time to come. And she hadn't dreamed of wedding bells and maternity, either.

Eventually they were able to retreat to the kitchen to wash the dishes while the others remained at the table, talking.

"We've made him unhappy," Melissa murmured, drying the dinner plate Kyle had just rinsed and washed. "All four of us."

"He'll get over it. Just give him some time."

"You handled him well, Kyle. I hope he didn't make you too uncomfortable."

"It was fine. I knew it was only because he loves you." He handed her another plate. "Telling my mother and brother will be easier."

"Mmm. When did you want to do that?"

"As soon as possible, though it's too late on the East Coast tonight. Are you free tomorrow afternoon?"

She nodded.

"I can leave the clinic a little early. Why don't you come over around five and we'll call them together."

KYLE'S MOTHER DIDN'T CARE about the sudden shift from friends to fiancés. Didn't even question it. She was every bit as thrilled as he'd thought she would be.

"My goodness, I can't believe it! That's fantastic news!"

Kyle held the receiver away from his ear so Melissa could hear his mother's effusions. Melissa's eyes widened and he winked at her, amused. Hadn't she known how much his mother liked her? They'd certainly gotten along well whenever his mother came to visit.

"I'm glad you're pleased," he said.

"Pleased? You couldn't have made me happier. It's about time you two settled down together. I've been waiting years for this."

"Oh, you have, have you?" It wasn't a big secret, he told himself. He'd already guessed how she felt. She asked after Melissa almost every time they talked. So why the strange expanding sensation in his chest? He motioned to Melissa. "Here, I'm putting her on." He handed her the cordless phone and went into his bedroom to pick up the extension.

"It's awfully romantic," Ellen Davenport was saying, "the way you were best friends first. You've really had a chance to get to know each other."

"Yes, we have," Melissa said.

Kyle sat down on the edge of his bed. "Mom, there's something else we need to tell you."

"Oh? What's that?"

"You're going to be a grandmother again."

AN HOUR LATER they finished their second phone call, this one to Kyle's brother. Craig was just as happy for them, though he did give Kyle a hard time for holding out on him when they'd talked on Saturday.

Their mother insisted on flying out for the wedding. Craig said he would try but wasn't sure if he could adjust his schedule. Regardless, they all decided that after the birth in April Kyle and Melissa would bring their baby to Massachusetts for a visit.

"We'll need to tell our friends soon," Melissa said. She'd joined him in his bedroom while they talked on the phone, taking the armchair in the corner. "Especially people like Barbara and Whitney—who know us both. Think they'll be shocked?"

He leaned forward as he sat on the bed, resting his forearms on his knees. Their faces were only a few feet apart. "I think they'll be happy for us."

Jesus, I'm *almost happy for us. Am I getting too carried away?* he wondered.

The thought planted a seed of anxiety inside him. This experience was too familiar. Six years ago...

But that had been different, he told himself. That had been his single attempt at a normal marriage. This wouldn't be the same. This would just be a very practical arrangement with a good friend. Thank God.

"You'll have to give notice to your landlord," she said.

"Already did. I'm officially out at the end of November. That'll allow us a few extra weeks to move my stuff over."

Strange that they would be living together within a month. Last week if someone had told him the future, he would have said they were insane.

Melissa cleared her throat. "I'll clean out the spare room. It already has a bed in it, so there's no rush to move yours. You'll have to bring your dresser, though. Anita took hers when she moved out."

"What's the plan when friends come over?"

"I guess we'll just close the bedroom doors. No one needs to know."

"Okay."

Melissa got up. She went to the nightstand and lined up a stack of books he'd left there. Then she crossed to the dresser, where a drawer was sticking out, and slid it back in. She touched the picture of him and Felicity, moving it sideways a few inches until it was perfectly centered on the top of the dresser.

She'd gone into cleaning mode, and she would hate it if he pointed it out to her. Obviously something had unnerved her. Kyle wondered if it was the same issue that was on his mind.

He waited until she ran out of steam, then he took her arm and pulled until she sat down on the bed—the bed where, last July, they'd made love, he couldn't help thinking.

"I need to level with you," he said. "I've never slept around, but I've also had a fairly active sex life. I don't particularly want to be celibate for the next twenty years."

She swallowed visibly. "God, Kyle. How can I keep up with this?" Her face had grown flushed. She frowned, staring down at her hands. "You want us just to...to...?"

Hop into bed.

No, that wasn't what he wanted, either. Mentally. But physically...?

She was a very attractive woman. He wouldn't be human if he didn't feel desire for her, especially with the memory of the night they'd shared, the sexy scent of gardenia, permanently burned into his brain. He wanted her this very moment, could feel the arousal building in his body.

"I don't want you to misunderstand. I'm not saying you have to do anything you don't want to do. I'm just saying it's something we should think about. If we're married for the next twenty years, or even for the rest of our lives, we might want to make love at some point."

The way we did last summer.

Her brown eyes flickered, her lashes drifting briefly downward as she came to terms with his words, and Kyle wanted, more than anything, to kiss her.

That was possibly the worst moment for a kiss. But he couldn't help it.

He tugged her onto his lap, as he had the other night when she'd been so upset. Pressing his lips to the warm, seductive spot behind her ear, he drank in the scent of her. He kissed her throat.

"What do you think you're doing?" she whispered.

"Reminding you that you're attracted to me."

Kyle heard her catch her breath when he ran his tongue along her collarbone. He worked his way back up her neck, kissed her jaw, drew closer to her mouth.

"I hadn't forgotten," she admitted. And she turned her head for his kiss.

Kyle didn't keep it mellow this time. He teased her with openmouthed kisses, then slipped his tongue between her lips. He let his hand drift up to the curve of her breast, and she arched her back in a way that drove him crazy.

Their tongues caressed each other with painstaking slowness. Lazy and sexy, but definitely not mellow. Their breathing quickened and soon they both shook with arousal. His unsteady fingers grazed the tip of her breast through the fabric of her shirt. She shuddered.

He backed off a little, kissed her cheekbone and then her eyelids. He drew in a rough, shaky breath.

"If you hadn't forgotten about this attraction,"

he said, hearing the hoarseness of his voice, "then what's so bad about making love?"

The second the words left his lips he realized he sounded like a randy sixteen-year-old.

And he could feel the tension in her body. He'd just asked the kind of pushy, pressuring question that would send her running.

Intimacy scared her. It scared him, too, of course, but he was a guy....

He made an exception when it came to the physical kind.

"Look," he said. "I'm sorry. I didn't mean for it to come out like that."

She scooted off his lap and sat beside him on the bed. "It's okay."

She was a little too calm to be believable.

It was as if nothing were wrong. As if nothing had happened. As if he hadn't been an overeager jerk and it hadn't flipped her out the least bit.

The wall was firmly in place. It had always existed between them, he realized—that familiar buffer that allowed them to be such comfortable companions but at the same time oddly sealed off from each other. Protected from getting too close.

And he didn't know what to do about it. Didn't know if he *wanted* to do anything about it. It made things easier to deal with.

It made their marriage a possibility.

He ran a hand through his hair. "What happened just now. I wasn't thinking. I shouldn't have kissed you.'' He took a deep breath. ''I'll give you more time,'' he promised. ''I won't rush you.''

LONG AFTER SHE LEFT, Kyle lay on his bed with the lights on, staring at the ceiling. The next several months, he suspected, would include some very frustrated, very unfulfilled nights.

CHAPTER SEVEN

MELISSA HADN'T EXPECTED to see Kyle again before her volunteer shift on Wednesday. Tuesday morning, however, found her pulling open the glass door of the clinic and stepping into the warmth of the lobby.

Whitney had classes on Tuesdays. The man at the receptionist's desk was someone Melissa had never met.

Melissa smiled at him and pointed toward the back. "I'm here to see Kyle. He's around, right?"

"He's in his office." The man glanced down at the console in front of him. "I think he might be on the phone."

Melissa shrugged. "I'll go back and wait." *He won't mind. He's going to marry me. He can't mind.*

She headed toward the rear. Barbara stood in the hallway, getting supplies out of a cupboard. Melissa could hear Kyle on the phone through his open office door.

Barbara caught sight of her. "Hey, girl. It's not Wednesday."

"I know. I'm just here for a visit."

"Care to see a couple of patients while you wait?"

"Uh, no, thanks." She and Kyle had planned to tell Barbara about their engagement on Wednesday, but she couldn't see the woman and not say something. "By the way," she said, "are you free next Friday evening?"

Barbara laughed. "I'm always free Friday evenings."

"Good," she said. "You can come to my wedding."

Barbara, never caught at a loss for anything, blinked. Her mouth worked. The only thing that came out was, "Holy cow."

"Yeah. No kidding. I feel the same way sometimes."

"Holy cow."

"You said that."

She blinked again. "Who?"

Suppressing a smile at Barbara's reaction, Melissa jerked her thumb toward Kyle's office.

"Melissa, that's wonderful." Barbara closed the distance between them and hugged Melissa against her. "And I'm going to kill him for not telling me."

"After the wedding, please."

Barbara released her. "Why? You got a baby that needs a name? Oh, Nelly. You do, don't you?"

Melissa nodded.

"The father...? It's...?"

"Him," she confirmed.

"You mean we're going to have a little Kyle-baby yelling down the place?"

"Yeah."

Barbara shook her head, smiling. "I *knew* something was going on between the two of you."

It all hit Melissa again. The enormity of it. She kept smiling back at Barbara. "Something happened, all right."

I'm going to love this baby, she reminded herself. *I can handle it, because I have to.*

Kyle came out into the hallway. He leaned against the wall. Barbara saw him. She strode over and punched him in the arm.

"Ouch."

"That's for keeping secrets."

"Sorry," he said, grinning.

She hugged him. A big Barbara hug. "Whitney doesn't know, does she?"

"Not yet. We'll tell her soon."

"You better." Barbara went off down the hall. Over her shoulder she said, "Because she and I are going to do some major gossiping about this."

Kyle ushered Melissa into his office. "Give me two minutes, okay?"

He sat down behind his desk and started leafing through a file folder. Paperwork was everywhere.

Melissa took a moment to look at him. Really look. *Her future husband.*

So much had changed since the last time she'd seen him in his office. Then she'd known he was the father of her child, but she'd never even dreamed they would decide to get married. That they would share their lives for the next eighteen years or more.

Kyle jotted some notes on a piece of paper in the file folder. Then he put the file away and looked up at her, smiling.

A very familiar smile. Not any different from the smile he'd given her last week, before he'd known he was a father. Before they'd agreed to marry.

Well, of course it was the same, she told herself. They were still friends, just as before. Only the fact that they were parents was different.

"So what's up?" Kyle asked.

"I'm not a hundred percent sure you're going to like this."

"Fire away."

"My dad called this morning. He said he'd talked with Father Martin. They have an opening on Friday evening. Next Friday evening. For a wedding."

"They?"

"My father's church."

"That's what I thought." He paused. "Did we talk about having a courthouse wedding?"

She nodded. "We did. But not with my father."

"And he assumed…"

"Yeah."

They stared at each other for a while. She was glad Kyle seemed to be taking it fairly well. Finally he smiled. "I'm not Catholic."

She smiled back. "I had noticed that."

"But you are."

She shrugged. "More or less."

"Mmm-hmm. I did have my heart set on a courthouse wedding...."

She knew he was teasing, trying to make this easy on her. Being his usual relaxed self. And she appreciated it.

She said, "It seems to be important to him."

Kyle tapped his fingers on the surface of his desk. He met her eyes. "And how do you feel about it?"

She hesitated. This was what had been bothering her for the past hour. A church wedding put a whole different spin on their marriage of convenience.

"Maybe I'm overreacting," she said, "but it feels a little off."

"You could put your foot down."

She could. But that would only confuse her father. Upset him. Possibly raise his suspicions. Why *shouldn't* she want to be married in a Catholic ceremony?

"I don't think so," she said.

"I could always refuse to marry you in a church," Kyle suggested.

"That would certainly endear you to him."

"Hey, I got his daughter pregnant. How much lower can I sink?"

She couldn't speak for a moment. *I got his daughter pregnant*. Still a shock to hear such words. Still so surreal. But she had to get used to their new situation. Get over her disbelief.

"There's lower," she assured him. "Believe me, there's lower."

Kyle smiled, but then his expression grew serious. "I'm okay with a church wedding. But if you don't want it, I'll stand behind you. We don't have to do anything that makes you uncomfortable."

Except marry each other.

"Remember who we're getting married for," he added.

"Yeah. My father."

Kyle shook his head. "Our baby. Our baby, who will definitely *not* be around for the wedding ceremony. Exactly how we choose to get married is not a big deal. The fact that we do, well, that's pretty big."

"I think the priest is going to want to talk to us. Beforehand."

Kyle shrugged. "We'll just have to pull the wool over his eyes, too."

MELISSA SLEPT POORLY that night.

She dreamed of getting married nine months

pregnant, of giving birth on the steps outside right after the ceremony.

And other, more frightening dreams. Dreams that woke her shaking in the early dawn. That teased at the edges of her brain, not coming into focus.

Blood.

Whose, she didn't know.

She lay there, paralyzed. Wretched.

In the bathroom, she threw up into the toilet. Mechanically she turned on the shower. Got under the stream of water because that's what you did. Faced her day because there were places she had to be, things she had to say, people she had to fix.

The water washed her clean. Clean enough, at least.

A church wedding was what her mother would have wanted.

BY THE TIME she went to the clinic she felt almost normal. After her shift they all went out for a celebratory dinner. At the *pho* shop, of course. Barbara and Whitney ribbed her and Kyle about their secret love affair but seemed genuinely happy for them.

And then she and Kyle went home.

To his place, as if nothing had changed. As if it were just any Wednesday night.

She kept herself together, as tight as ever. Neatly packaged. She had put her feelings from the morning behind her. Feelings she hadn't tried to understand, hadn't let herself understand.

Feelings that just happened sometimes. Longing and loss.

Nothing she could share.

They watched television on his couch. She watered the ficus. They didn't talk about the future. She didn't want to open it up, though the subject crossed her mind a hundred times.

Little things. Where they would put his television, and the rest of the objects from his apartment when he moved in with her.

This move required change. And it was that change, among everything else, that scared her. Unnerved her.

Their show ended. Mulder and Scully had faced down their opponent in their characteristically emotionless way. Good had not triumphed over evil, but neither had evil won out.

They walked to her bungalow through the cool October air. At her door, with Kyle ready to leave, she said, "What are you going to wear?"

Because it's not just Wednesday night. It's almost our last Wednesday night as the people we used to be. We have to think about what's coming.

She didn't have to explain the question any further. He understood.

"A suit," he said. "You?"

"I don't know. Something."

Her mother's dress was packed away in a big

white box in the basement at her dad's house. She'd looked at the dress once when she was twelve. It felt soft, like her mother's face.

Church wedding.

The idea overwhelmed her. *Oh, God, help me.*

She thought of Kyle's questions the night she'd told him about the baby. *Who do you turn to, Melissa?*

But who did you turn to when you couldn't talk at all?

She said, "I have a doctor's appointment tomorrow. Routine pregnancy exam. Do you want to come?"

"Yes," he said. "Yes."

DR. NATALIE PORTER was in her late forties, a slim woman with jet-black hair. She gave an immediate impression of inner calm and extreme competence. Kyle warmed to her right away.

Dr. Porter greeted them both with a smile. "Still no morning sickness, Melissa?"

"Not really."

"Everything else going okay?"

"Yeah, things are fine."

Satisfied, she tilted her head Kyle's way. "The father?"

"Yes," Melissa said.

Kyle introduced himself.

"He runs the free clinic downtown," Melissa explained. "We're getting married."

Dr. Porter smiled. "Have you known each other long?"

"Five years," Melissa said.

"Are you staying for the exam?" the doctor asked him.

He looked at Melissa. This was her call.

"Yes," she said.

"You know the drill, then. Out of the clothes and into the gown. I'll be right back."

Kyle walked over to the window so Melissa would have privacy to change. Dr. Porter's offices were on the twelfth floor of the professional building adjacent to the hospital. From the exam room Kyle looked down on the hospital and beyond it to the Willamette River, curving past downtown.

Behind him he could hear the rustle of her clothing as she removed it, the crackle of the paper gown as she put it on.

Briefly he felt that this was too intimate.

But he appreciated her willingness to share the whole experience of having a baby with him.

"I'm decent," she told him. "And anyway," she added after he'd turned around, "it's just my body."

And I'm a doctor, she didn't add. *So this isn't about sex, or intimacy, or us. It's just about our baby.*

Dr. Porter came back into the room. She began to perform the exam, asking questions while she did so. Diet, exercise, general bodily changes.

"Any cramping or spotting?" she inquired as she palpated Melissa's abdomen.

"None."

"You're having a pretty easy pregnancy so far," the doctor observed.

"Physically," Melissa said.

"How about emotionally?"

"It's an adjustment."

Dr. Porter glanced over at him, assessing, insightful, and he felt for some reason that she'd seen far more than he wanted her to. Then she turned back to Melissa. "Pregnancy is an adjustment even for couples who've been *trying* to have a baby. When it's a surprise and creates other changes in your life…well, it's natural for it to feel challenging."

She motioned Kyle over. "Let me show you what's going on here." She explained how she could determine the size of the uterus by palpation, and how they would track its height throughout the pregnancy to make sure the baby was growing properly.

He watched, fascinated. The exam made the baby seem much more real. Much more overwhelming. In about six months he would have a son or daughter to love, feed, nurture and educate. The responsibility was daunting.

"What do you know about babies?" Dr. Porter asked him.

"Next to nothing." And that was something he would have to remedy immediately.

Melissa said, "I have some books at home."

"I'll read them."

MELISSA DROVE to Anita's apartment that evening after work. They'd arranged to have dinner together to go over details for the wedding.

"Sometimes it feels as if I'm not even pregnant," she told Anita when they were settled in her kitchen, eating stir-fried vegetables and tofu with brown rice. Troy was at work and wouldn't be home until late that night. "And then I'll remember that I am and it hits me all over again."

"I'm having a hard time forgetting."

"Oh, the morning sickness."

"Yeah. You have no idea how lucky you are."

Melissa grinned. "Maybe I'll have a really long and painful labor."

"With my luck I will, too. Are you going to have natural childbirth?"

"I want to," Melissa answered. "If everything is okay."

Anita shivered. "I don't think I'd be able to handle that. I'll probably be having a huge anxiety attack anyway. I worry a lot that something will go wrong."

"With the birth?"

"With everything."

"I'm sure it'll be okay."

"I didn't stop painting with oils until I knew I was pregnant," she said, the words rushed as if they were a confession.

Melissa knew oil painting involved fumes and volatile chemicals, but she also knew her sister was careful with them. As long as Anita hadn't made herself sick she probably hadn't hurt the developing embryo.

"I'm sure a lot of mothers have painted," Melissa said. "And you're doing all the right things now. Look at what we're eating..."

"Hey, I *like* brown rice," Anita said. "Oh, I forgot to tell you. Dad's coming over in a little while to help us with wedding plans."

"Really?"

"Yeah. I think he wants to take care of the stuff Mom would have. He's really happy that you're getting married, you know."

"And how are you with it?"

"Oh, I love weddings," Anita said. "Just not my own. Yet."

When their father arrived he had their mother's wedding dress with him. He put it down on the coffee table in the living room. "You're about the same size she was," he told her.

Melissa's chest contracted.

Her mother's dress.

She remembered that one time she'd seen it. Sneaking down into the basement to the corner where her father kept her mother's things. Guiltily peering inside the white paperboard box. Touching the fabric.

Anita opened the box. Melissa wondered if her sister had ever snuck down to the basement the way she had and hidden away to spend a moment with her memories of their mother.

Anita unfolded the dress and held it out in front of her. "It's beautiful," she said.

She turned it so it faced Melissa and their father.

In his bedroom there were pictures of him and their mother on their wedding day. But seeing the dress close up, unfolded, was something else.

It was exquisite, with intricate beadwork on the bodice and beautiful lines.

"Try it on," her father said.

A feeling of panic took hold of Melissa. It seemed to twist her stomach upon itself.

"Come on," Anita said. "I'll help you."

They went into Anita's bedroom. Anita laid the dress out on the bed.

"I don't know if I can do this," Melissa confessed. She almost wanted to cry but didn't.

Anita gave her a quick hug. "I know it's sad. But I think it's what she would have wanted."

It was the one reason to do it that Melissa couldn't ignore. She took off her clothes.

Anita helped her pull on the dress and fastened the tiny hooks running up the back. "There," she said. "Finished. Turn around."

Her feet felt unconnected to her body. "How does it look?"

"Oh, my." That was all Anita said, all she needed to say. Melissa could feel that the dress fit perfectly, even with the slight changes in her body from pregnancy.

The only mirror in Anita's bedroom was a small one on the wall. It showed Melissa only from her face to her stomach. Melissa stared for a long moment, seeing her mother's image from the pictures on her father's wall.

"Let's go show Dad," Anita said.

CHAPTER EIGHT

KYLE HAD LUNCH at Buddy's before meeting Melissa at the church for their prewedding interview. He went almost every Friday for the rice-and-bean special, with corn bread that was to die for. He would have happily paid five dollars for it, instead of the buck twenty-five they charged.

He ordered his food and took his plastic number to a stool at the counter to wait for it to be dished up. A thirty-five-year-old woman missing most of her teeth served him a glass of iced tea.

When his meal arrived he was surprised to see who delivered it. The kid who'd come into the clinic a week ago.

"Hey, Blue," he said.

It took a second for the kid to recognize him. "Oh, hey," he said. "Thanks again for that stuff." He put down Kyle's meal and gave him a fork wrapped in a napkin.

"No problem. You're working here now?"

"Yeah, in the job-training program."

"Good move," Kyle said. The job-training program at Buddy's offered people a chance to work for their meals and earn a few dollars a day. With a reference from this place Blue might be able to land a regular restaurant job and start getting his feet underneath him.

He noticed Blue wasn't wearing the splint anymore. "How's the arm?"

"Better. You need anything else?"

"No, I'm good."

Blue went off to serve more plates of food, and Kyle dug into his rice and beans. He struck up a conversation with the guy on the stool next to his, and after the meal he chatted briefly with a few of the administrative employees in the upstairs loft above the restaurant. The nonprofit community in Old Town was small and closely knit.

He told the director, a friend of his, about his wedding plans.

"Melissa Lopez, huh?" the woman said. "I've met her, right? You've brought her in here a couple of times."

"Showing her the highlights of the neighborhood...."

"Kind of sudden."

He didn't want to get into things right now, though the truth would be evident soon. "Yeah, well," he said, smiling and easy, "when I decide I want something I don't like to waste time."

THE PRIEST'S OFFICE in the church was a darkpaneled room. Kyle glanced around. The wood was so brown it looked almost black. Heavy books sat on the shelves behind Father Martin's desk. One narrow window looked out onto a small courtyard, into which the October rain pattered.

"I understand there's some urgency for this wedding," the priest commented after the introductions had been made. His tone was warm and a little wry, not critical. Obviously this was not the first time he'd encountered a situation like theirs.

"Yes, there is," Kyle said.

The priest's attitude made him feel more comfortable. Despite what he'd said to Melissa at his office, he'd realized it did feel strange to be getting married in a church. A civil ceremony with a judge had seemed much more in line with the arrangement they were making.

"And the baby is due...?"

"Mid-April," Melissa supplied.

The priest nodded. "Six months yet. Good. That will give the two of you a chance to settle into married life together." He paused, steepling his fingers under his chin. "Have you been married before, Kyle? I know Melissa hasn't."

"No," he said. He didn't volunteer that he'd been engaged once.

Father Martin nodded. "Often the very young couples who come in here have no idea what marriage is really like, the sacrifices it demands. You two are both older, more mature. But sometimes that presents problems of its own. You might be more set in your ways, more accustomed to the freedom of living alone.'' He paused, inviting comment.

''I'm sure we'll adjust,'' Melissa said. ''We've known each other a long time.''

''Your father said you've been friends for a while.''

''Yes.''

''It's a tricky situation,'' he said after another thoughtful pause. ''With a baby on the way. I applaud you, though, for doing what's right for the child. I'm sure it will be the right decision for the two of you, as well.''

''Yes,'' Melissa repeated.

The priest pursed his lips. ''Is the marriage freely chosen? Do either of you have reservations?''

Kyle looked at Melissa, whose gaze was focused on the priest. He suspected they both had reservations. Serious ones. But they didn't count. There was one choice to make, and they had made it.

''No,'' he announced.

''REMIND ME WHY we're doing this,'' Anita said as she parked her little car in a ''compact only'' spot in a downtown parking garage.

''I'm looking for a dress.''

It was Tuesday. Only a few days before her sister's wedding. Anita locked the car and walked beside Melissa to the elevator.

Other people were waiting, so they didn't speak

more until they were out on the street. "You already have a dress," she said.

"You know how I feel about wearing Mom's dress."

"Conflicted." They crossed the street and entered a one-block-square shopping mall with four levels of stores. "Of course you do. That's only natural."

"So humor me."

Anita humored her. They went to a bridal store on the top floor of the mall. "Nothing poofy, right?"

"Exactly," Melissa said.

Anita eyed the racks of dresses. "How about something slinky, then? You've got the figure for it."

Melissa blew her breath out in a sigh. "At this point, all I really care about are a few simple words and a ring."

"Gotcha." She went to a rack and flipped through the dresses. "Here's one," she said. "Basic, classy."

As she held it out for Melissa, she felt a twinge in her abdomen. "Ooh."

Melissa's eyes went to her face. "What's wrong?"

The twinge passed as quickly as it had come on; the panic it had created didn't. But she tried to push it back, ignore it. "I don't know. Just a gas pain or something."

"You're okay?"

"Yeah. Here, do you like this one?"

Melissa eyed the dress. "It's okay," she said.

"Try it on," Anita encouraged.

When Melissa went into the changing room, Anita allowed herself to indulge in a moment of worry. Worry that she would lose the baby. That her painting, or the medication she took for her anxiety, or her anxiety itself, had done some kind of irreparable damage. Despite Melissa's and Dr. Porter's reassurances.

Something just felt wrong inside. The twinge was back. She could feel it if she focused on it. And it was almost impossible not to focus on it.

Melissa came out of the changing room in the dress. It looked good, but it wasn't anything special.

"What do you think?" Melissa asked.

"It's okay," Anita said, honest.

"That's what I think. And a little too expensive for just being okay."

"Let's keep hunting, then."

Melissa said, "You know, I've probably got something in my closet at home that would look just fine."

"And you've got Mom's dress," Anita reminded her. "It's beautiful, it fits and the price can't be beat."

Melissa didn't appear convinced.

WHEN SHE AND KYLE CAME HOME that Wednesday after their regular dinner with Barbara and Whitney, Melissa parked outside his apartment.

As usual, she thought. Everything was so normal.

But then Kyle said, "Why don't we watch at your place?"

Unexpected.

It shouldn't have been a jolt, but it was. She wanted to say no, because that was for after Friday. After the wedding. She'd paced it all out, had told herself that by then she would be ready.

But how long could you forestall the inevitable? And what difference would it make to do so?

"My television," she said. "It's too small."

"I'll bring mine over."

She said nothing.

"It has to happen sometime."

No, it didn't. They could just keep things the same. Watch television on her tiny set. Or keep paying rent on his apartment, and watch it there every Wednesday night.

"Fine," she said. "Bring it over."

"You're upset."

"Hormones," she said, making excuses. "Change."

"Forget it, then. Come up. We'll watch here."

"It's okay," she said. "I have to face this." The loss of her security, her safety zone, the buffer she kept around herself.

They went upstairs and unplugged his television set from the wall and the VCR. Kyle carried it with the glass against his chest, sidling out the front door. They took the elevator.

"Should we drive around the corner?" she asked.

Kyle shrugged. "It'll probably be more trouble than it's worth to get it in and out of the car."

Outside, she looked at the size of the door openings and compared it with the television in Kyle's arms. "You're right."

"It's not that far," Kyle said.

And he was strong. He carried the big television set easily, not even breathing hard. As if it were a paper sack of groceries.

Inside the bungalow he put the TV down and unhooked hers. Then placed the small television in the spare room, on the floor. Its cord trailed across the hardwood.

While Kyle went back into the living room, Melissa bent to coil the cord. She tucked it neatly away. The set wasn't worthless, she told herself, just because his TV was bigger.

"Did I tell you I saw Zita today?" Kyle called from the living room.

She walked out of the spare room. Kyle was kneeling, hooking his TV to her VCR. "No."

"She's got a dog. A little three-legged Chihuahua."

Zita with a dog? "I never saw her as a pet person."

"Neither did I. She said she found it in a box by a Dumpster across the river. I guess someone needed his pet to be perfect."

Kyle stood. The television was all hooked up. He turned it on.

The volume seemed loud, though it had been fine at his place. The machine itself looked monstrous. Far too big for the tiny table it sat on.

The *X-Files* episode that night was about a man-creature who fed on human livers. Melissa had to leave the room.

"I'm sorry," she said when he turned off the television and came to the kitchen doorway. She leaned against the counter next to the stove, sipping tea. He put his weight against the door frame.

"What's up?" he asked.

"I can't watch."

It was pregnancy, she told herself. The cause of these feelings that didn't make sense, that didn't let her behave as she wanted to.

"Okay…"

She'd never walked away from an *X-Files* episode before. She was a doctor, damn it. Monsters and gore didn't faze her. Nor did blood, except in her own nightmares.

She sensed the fear in herself.

Of getting attached. Of losing him. Of this all

ending with his blood on her body, just as it had with her mother and brother.

She couldn't handle that. Didn't want to have to face it.

"I'm sorry," he said.

You rushed me.

"We should have watched at my place. I shouldn't have brought my set over."

You rushed me.

"All this can wait until after we're married."

"Okay," she said, wanting him to leave so she could be alone in her house with his big television set.

"I rushed you," he said.

She stared at him, wondering if she'd conjured the words or imagined him saying them.

"I told you I wouldn't," he continued, "but I did… This is hard. For both of us. I'll leave the rest of my stuff for later. Afterward. There's plenty of time before I have to clear out my apartment."

"Okay," she said again, wanting more than ever for him to leave. Not able to handle his understanding. His Kyle brand of empathy. His friendship.

SHE SHOWED UP at the church in a white dress.

Kyle took one look and knew it must be her mother's, both from the old-fashioned styling and from the fact that Melissa would never have bought such a formal gown for a marriage of convenience.

He didn't know what he'd expected. Something simple. A plain dress in some muted but attractive color.

Not this.

She looked amazing. Melissa *always* looked amazing, even when she lounged around the house in sweats. But this was a particular kind of amazing. Not radiant, exactly, because this wedding of necessity didn't call forth that kind of emotion. But as close as you could get.

She started toward him on her father's arm. Suddenly the church seemed too small, despite its high arched ceiling, the long aisle.

He was only faintly aware of the ornate carvings that decorated the walls, the candles that burned by the altar, giving off a soft glow.

He was thinking of another wedding. One that had never taken place. He and Felicity were to have been married in the Episcopal Cathedral in Boston, in front of hundreds of people. It would have been a big deal. An event.

He had looked forward to it.

His gut twisted a little. After Felicity's death he'd seen her dress. Her parents had shown it to him. He couldn't really remember what it had looked like.

Damn it. This wasn't the time to think about the past. About what was supposed to have been.

No, think about reality. Marriage to Melissa.

Kyle couldn't regret their decision. Couldn't regret this ceremony.

He would be a good father to their child.

Had to be.

HALFWAY UP THE AISLE, walking past the empty pews, Melissa saw the tears on her father's cheeks.

She squeezed his arm, giving him support.

His wide, handsome face was calm, not contorted with emotion. And there were only a couple of tears.

But still.

She knew her father was crying for her mother, wishing she could be here on her daughter's wedding day. Melissa had had the same painful thought herself more than once recently.

Even though this wasn't a real marriage.

And especially when she'd decided to wear her mother's dress after all.

She'd convinced herself that to buy a new wedding dress—or wear something from the back of her closet—would be too hard on her father. Her reluctance to wear the dress involved more than just sadness at losing her mother, but she couldn't explain that to him.

So she'd put on the dress. She could tell it had made him happy, despite his tears now.

They stopped at the top of the aisle. Her father kissed her on the cheek. He summoned a smile. "I'm so happy for you," he whispered.

"Thanks, Dad," she said. "I love you, too."

And then she stepped forward to meet Kyle. Her sister and Kyle's friend Jerome stood as their attendants. Craig hadn't been able to make it, so Jerome had filled in.

Melissa gazed at her husband-to-be, the man who would be her partner in this strange arrangement.

Kyle looked good. He wore a dark-brown suit. A familiar suit, she realized, from a cancer-research charity dinner they'd attended together a year earlier. She didn't have many opportunities to observe him in formal clothes, but she had to admit they flattered him. Made him appear particularly handsome and competent and in charge of his own destiny.

At the moment she did *not* feel particularly in control of her own destiny. The enormity of what she was about to do struck her yet again.

Getting married.

Father Martin started the service. He read briefly from the New Testament and gave a short homily.

As he talked, Kyle shot her a small smile. *It'll be okay,* the smile seemed to say. *We know why we're here, and it's the right thing to do.*

Father Martin paused for a moment, then began the wedding ceremony itself. He asked them, "Melissa and Kyle, have you come here freely and without reservation to give yourselves to each other in marriage?"

They both said yes, but Melissa was thinking, *only because there was no other choice. Because it was the only solution.*

He asked, "Will you love and honor each other as husband and wife for the rest of your lives?"

She said yes, mentally substituting "like" for "love."

He asked, "Will you accept children lovingly from God, and bring them up to the best of your abilities?"

We already have, and that's the whole point of this exercise.

At Father Martin's direction, they took each other's hands. The priest asked, "Do you, Kyle, take Melissa to be your wife? Do you promise to be true to her in good times and bad, in sickness and in health, to love her and honor her all the days of your life?"

Kyle said, "I do," in that wonderfully smooth voice of his. He smiled calmly down at her.

Everything's okay. It's mellow. We've just made a businesslike arrangement. It's no big deal. Our friendship will see us through.

The priest turned to Melissa and asked the same question. Even as he began to speak, Melissa felt a shiver up and down her spine. Could she be true to Kyle in good times and bad, in sickness and in health? Sure, she could. That part was easy.

The other part was what challenged her. Her mind seemed to edit out the other words and left her with the phrase *Do you promise to love him?* resounding in her head. It repeated over and over, echoing.

"Melissa?" the priest prompted.

Do you promise to love him?

She yanked herself back to reality. "I do," she said, automatically.

And then it struck her.

Oh, good God Almighty.

The chapel blurred for a moment. Old stone and mahogany gave an overpowering impression of darkness, even with afternoon light streaming in through the stained-glass windows high on the walls.

Kyle's face wavered, then reformed.

She loved him.

Oh, good God Almighty, she loved him.

This marriage wasn't a fraud after all. Not for her. She really loved him. She stood there in her mother's wedding dress in her father's church, and she loved Kyle Davenport.

The only fraud was the one she'd perpetrated on herself. Telling herself she could go through the motions of a regular marriage and not feel any of the regular emotions.

Father Martin looked over at Anita and Jerome. "Do you have the rings?"

The two stepped forward with the rings. The priest blessed them. Melissa took Kyle's ring. Her fingers trembled a bit as she slipped the heavy gold band onto Kyle's finger. "Take this ring," she said, "as a sign of my love and fidelity."

And she meant it.

She stared at the gold encircling Kyle's finger. The gold she'd put there.

They'd picked out matching gold bands at a downtown jeweler's. A simple style, designed to be comfortable and unobtrusive. The kind that registered the commitment but didn't attract any undue attention.

He hadn't bought her an engagement ring.

She didn't mind. With a baby coming they had more important places to spend their money.

Theirs was supposed to be a practical arrangement.

Theirs was a marriage of convenience.

A crashing sense of despair hit her.

I love you, she thought. *And I've just bound myself to you.*

Oh, no.

Unaware of her inner turmoil, Kyle slipped her ring onto her finger. He said the same words she had.

Melissa stared up into his eyes. He smiled calmly back at her, as if he'd just made some inane comment about the weather.

The wedding ceremony was exactly what they'd planned. Mellow, easygoing. They were two friends doing the right thing for their baby.

But she'd blown it. Somewhere along the line she'd fallen in love with Kyle. With *Kyle*, of all people.

Oh, hell.

CHAPTER NINE

AFTER THE WEDDING they went to her father's favorite restaurant, which happened to be a few blocks from the church. They occupied a private dining room in the back and ate a delicious meal of Italian food, which Melissa barely tasted.

No one noticed that she'd fallen in love.

"Where are you going on your honeymoon?" Whitney asked as a waiter brought out a beautiful wedding cake. Melissa had ordered it from her favorite bakery and had it delivered to the restaurant.

"Nowhere," Melissa said.

"Nowhere?" Barbara demanded.

"They're too busy right now," Kyle's mother explained.

Barbara glared good-naturedly at Kyle. "I don't know when you started thinking you were the center of the universe, but we *can* get along without you at the clinic for a day or two. Especially on the weekend. What's the story here—you don't love her enough to take her away somewhere?"

"I have to work all weekend," Melissa explained. "I'm saving my vacation hours for later in my pregnancy or for when the baby is born."

"I'll baby-sit," Whitney said, "anytime you want to go away."

Kyle's mom grinned at Whitney. "If I lived in Portland you'd have to fight me for that privilege."

"Who's ready for cake?" Kyle asked.

"I am," Melissa said, eager to get away from the subject of honeymoons.

The waiter put the cake on the table in front of her. She picked up the cake knife and got ready to make the first slice.

"Wait a second," Anita said. "Aren't you going to cut it together?"

Melissa looked at Kyle. "Are we?"

"Why not?"

She still held the knife. Kyle wrapped his hand around hers. His was large and warm. She felt all her awareness go to the skin on the back of hers, to the spaces between her fingers where his fingers had settled.

"Who in the world came up with these rituals?" he murmured. He was close to her, their bodies touching with the easy intimacy of longtime lovers. Her back was against his chest. His free hand rested on her shoulder as casually as if they touched that way every day.

When in truth they'd hardly ever touched. Not until recently. In the long span of their friendship they'd almost never had physical contact with each other, which was probably what had made that July night so explosive.

She felt overheated suddenly. Overaware.

And intertwined.

This wasn't what she'd wanted, not to this extent. But it was too late to go back. They were married. Her mind flashed forward to the moments they would have in their lives together. Sharing things. Raising a child in partnership, neither of them having full control, each always reacting to the other's actions as they carried out even the simplest tasks.

Each vulnerable to losing the other. Though it would matter more to her than to him, since he felt only friendly regard for her and she felt so much more.

With an effort Melissa pushed her thoughts aside and focused on cutting out a slice of cake. She and Kyle made two neat cuts and then slid the knife underneath the first piece to pull it from the cake. With her free hand Melissa steadied the piece as they brought it to a waiting plate.

There. The performance was done.

Kyle released her hand. She put down the knife, glad the contact was over.

But then Kyle picked up a fork and cut out a small chunk, complete with icing, which he took in his fingers and offered to her.

"You're really getting into this," she murmured as he held the cake out.

"When in Rome..." he said.

She took the bite from his fingers. Her lips

brushed his skin as she closed them. The contact was instantly and powerfully sexual.

It took her breath away. But even as she felt that, another part of her stood distant, observing.

You're eating from his hands, Melissa.

Where will it end?

She shivered, suddenly feeling very alone.

REALITY WAS HITTING HARD. Kyle put a good face on it. He laughed and joked and played the part of the happy bridegroom. But inside he felt incredibly uncomfortable.

Married. He was married now.

To Melissa. His closest friend.

And all he wanted to do was to take her somewhere private and make love to her. Which definitely wasn't part of their arrangement.

Not yet. If ever.

It was all so damned ironic, he thought as he ate cake and sipped coffee in the private dining room. They'd structured their friendship—both of them—so it wouldn't get too intense. But it had escaped their control. Not only in July, but this evening, too.

They'd gotten *married*.

God, he'd gotten himself in too deep, and there was no shallow water in sight. So he would just have to keep swimming, pretend everything was okay. Make the best of the situation.

AN HOUR LATER they pulled up outside her little blue bungalow.

Their little blue bungalow. Kyle already had his own key. For years now he'd kept a spare copy for her, in case she got locked out. But now it was really his key.

"We should put your name on the lease," she said. Knowing it wasn't the most romantic thing to say. Dead set on staying as far from romance as she could manage.

She felt jittery and uncomfortable. Even more so than she'd expected when Anita had picked her up a few hours ago to prepare for the wedding.

Kyle said, "Or skip that step and go straight to the offer to purchase."

Her white car was already parked in the driveway, so Kyle parked on the street.

Anita had driven her to the wedding; Kyle had driven her home.

It was simply one more strange transition on this uncomfortable day.

She'd ridden in Kyle's car a hundred times before. But never as his wife. And never knowing she loved him. That made it different. Painful.

They both stepped out of the car at the same time. She reached into the rear seat for her street clothes.

Kyle carried nothing. He had left his apartment in his suit, shown up at the church wearing it, and was now back in their neighborhood as if nothing had changed. Meanwhile, she had left her house in pants and a plain T-shirt. Had gone to Anita's house and let her sister fuss with her hair before changing and heading for the church. And was returning home in a beautiful wedding dress that had the power to make her feel incredibly sad.

He didn't carry her over the threshold. Instead they walked up the sidewalk together. He unlocked the door and let her step in first.

She entered her familiar living room. Except for the television, it was exactly as it always had been. Kyle would keep his personal belongings in the second bedroom. They hadn't yet sorted out the household items they would share, deciding what to keep and what to give away.

He smiled at her. "Feels weird, doesn't it?"

You could say that. She knew it was wrong to feel so threatened, to be so off balance. This was just Kyle. Her old friend Kyle.

"We'll get used to it," she assured him. Assured herself. As if saying it could make it so.

She went into the bedroom to change, and came out again a moment later, still in the dress. "I'm going to need some help," she admitted.

He followed her into the bedroom.

The bedroom that might someday be *their* bedroom.

Shaking slightly, she turned her back to him. Strong, sure fingers worked at the eyelets. She felt hot inside at the thought of him undressing her, seeing her bare back. His knuckles brushed her skin. The sensation was electric, and it made her want to turn in his arms, kiss him, drag him into bed.

But she knew she couldn't. Not in her current state. She would slip somehow, reveal her new-found feelings. And then everything would be more difficult than it already was.

''That's far enough,'' she said when he got to the middle of her back, below her shoulder blades. She reached around and confirmed that she could unfasten the hooks from there downward. ''Thanks.''

''No problem.'' He didn't leave.

''I'll—I'll see you in a minute,'' she said.

When he was safely out of the room and she had closed the door behind him she unfastened the dress and let it slip off her body.

She changed back into the pants and T-shirt she had worn earlier, then hung the dress neatly in her closet. Tomorrow she would fold it back into its box and return it to her father's house.

Kyle was in the living room when she came out. ''I'm making tea,'' she announced on her way into the kitchen. ''Want some?''

She poured water into the kettle and put it on the stove, then got the teapot ready. While the water heated she tidied the already clean kitchen. Wiped down the counters. Put a glass into the dishwasher. Refilled her water purifier.

She looked up to find Kyle lounging in the doorway, watching her. He'd taken off his coat and removed his tie. Even in a white shirt and the brown suit pants he looked good. His sleeves were rolled up to expose his forearms, the top button of his shirt undone. He looked casual. Relaxed.

"Something on your mind?" he asked.

"What? Oh, no. Just waiting for the water to boil."

As if on cue, the kettle started to warble. Melissa poured the water into her big glass teapot, over loose chamomile tea. The flowers and stems and leaves floated to the top of the strainer, then settled slowly to the bottom. One at a time at first, then more swiftly. Like the white particles in one of those snow globes, only darker.

Kyle walked across the kitchen. She heard his footfalls—a man's shoes with their heavy leather soles; they sounded loud in her ears. He stood next to her, and she picked up the scent of his body, warm and masculine. And sexy.

"Second thoughts?" he asked.

She turned to face him. "Yes." *But not for the reason you think.*

"That's natural. It's a big thing we did today."

"Yeah." She hesitated. "And strange."

He nodded.

"To be married without being in love."

"It's different," Kyle agreed.

"But it'll all work out okay, right? Because even if we don't love each other, we're good friends."

Stupid fool, she thought. *He's not going to contradict you. Not going to say, No, wait a minute— I do love you.*

She was the only one whose feelings had taken that turn. Kyle was still too haunted by what had happened with Felicity.

"We're doing the right thing," Kyle said. "And we'll work out all the details."

Details.

Such as sex.

He was too damned easygoing about sex, she thought. Too comfortable with the idea of continuing what had started in July.

Men were taught to be different from women, weren't they? Trained to be able to separate sex and love.

She couldn't. Not with him.

She poured two mugs of tea. "I know. It just feels like such a big change right now." Even the house felt small with him in it. Smaller than it had ever felt when she'd shared it with Anita.

"We'll get used to things. Give it time."

Melissa sipped her too-hot tea. She kept the mug in front of her mouth, hiding behind it, using it as a shield. She sipped again. The liquid burned her taste buds.

Neither of them spoke for a moment. She thought of the evening in front of them. It was too early to go to sleep, but she didn't know what they would do for the next couple of hours. She usually felt so comfortable with Kyle, but now things seemed awkward and uncertain.

Realizing you'd fallen in love with your friend could be unnerving. Particularly if that person had just married you for purely practical reasons.

"Maybe we should move some of your stuff over," she suggested, grasping at straws. "Do you have anything packed?"

He watched her. "Jerome was going to help me tomorrow afternoon. But we can get the process started."

They finished their tea and walked around the corner to his apartment.

"I'm not bringing everything," he said, waving a hand around the apartment.

"It would never fit."

They each took an armful of clothes from his closet and returned to the bungalow. The closet in the spare bedroom was empty. Melissa had removed the items she'd stored there after Anita had moved out. Kyle hung everything up, then they went back to his apartment.

To be doing something felt good, Melissa realized. It took away the awkwardness and reminded her why she and Kyle had become friends. Why she'd fallen in love with him.

"What else do you want to bring over?"

Kyle nodded toward the dresser. "That. But I was planning to do it tomorrow."

The dresser had five drawers, but it wasn't huge.

"We could do it tonight," Melissa said. "If we carry the drawers separately. The main part can't be that heavy."

He raised an eyebrow at her.

"I'm not a wimp, Kyle. You know that. And there's no reason I shouldn't be able to lift moderate weights."

"How about we try it?"

They pulled out the drawers and put them on top of the bed. As Kyle removed the fifth drawer, the deep bottom one with several pairs of pants and a couple of sweaters in it, Melissa picked up the photo of Felicity and him.

She held it in her hand. Couldn't help staring at it, though she'd seen it before. It showed Kyle and Felicity arm in arm in front of the wide trunk of a maple tree. They wore jeans and old, comfortable sweaters. In the background lay a pile of red and yellow leaves.

Kyle appeared younger. The two of them looked very much in love. Felicity seemed to glow with happiness. The photo had been taken in the fall, many months before the suicide. Had it been an unusually happy moment, Melissa wondered, or had their early months together been like that all the time?

Melissa put the photograph down on the bed.

It was *her* wedding day.

But the woman Kyle should have married, the woman he'd actually *wanted* to marry, stared back at her from Kyle's bed. From the very place she and Kyle had gotten themselves into this mess by making love.

"Ready?" he asked.

Melissa turned and found him watching her. His gaze took in the photograph, as well.

He didn't say anything.

She walked over to him. Kyle lifted the empty dresser and set it down a few feet out from the wall.

"Tip it toward me," he said. "Then you can pick up the bottom and see what you think."

It wasn't heavy at all, probably because it was made of real wood instead of particleboard, which weighed more.

"I can handle this," she said, "no problem."

"All the way around the corner?"

"You'll let me rest, right?"

"Of course."

"Then let's go. We can take the drawers over in one of our cars."

At the bungalow they set the empty shell of a dresser in the spare room. As Kyle nudged it into place, Melissa wondered whether he would put the picture on top of it again, and why she felt so jealous of a dead woman.

KYLE WOKE feeling disoriented. It took him a few seconds to realize why the paint was the wrong color and the windows were on the wrong walls.

This wasn't his bedroom.

But he didn't live around the corner anymore. He lived with Melissa in her bungalow. And they were married, though he was little more than the roommate she'd halfheartedly advertised for after Anita had moved out.

This *was* his bedroom now.

He pulled on his robe and knotted the belt, then he crossed to the nearest window, which looked out onto a narrow strip of side yard, a bit of grass edging a stone pathway to the back of the house. The neighbor's hedge on the other side of the wooden fence blocked the view beyond.

The other window, on the back wall, was much better. It had a full view of the garden and actually let in some light. Without his contacts the garden was blurry.

He'd told Melissa they would figure out all the details. But what if they never did? He wouldn't be her roommate for twenty years, kid or no kid. Unless they decided to have some kind of open marriage, where they could each have discreet relationships with other people. That, after all, was what it had been like to be friends with her.

In the bathroom he showered and shaved, just as if it were an ordinary morning. When he was dressed he found Melissa in the kitchen, chopping an onion.

"'Morning," he said.

She turned her head to look at him over her shoulder. "Hi."

If this had been a real marriage they would have spent the whole night making love. He would feel content and sated this morning instead of edgy. If this had been a real marriage he wouldn't have been relegated to the extra bedroom.

But it wasn't real.

"What are you making?"

"An omelette."

"Enough for two?"

She slid the onions into a pan that had been heating on the stove. They sizzled immediately. "Yes."

"Sounds delicious." He headed for the fridge to pour himself a glass of orange juice.

"But don't get the idea that I'm going to cook every meal for you. That's not what this arrangement is about."

His hand on the refrigerator door, Kyle looked over at her. She had her back to him as she stirred the onions with a wooden spoon. Stiff posture. Tight shoulders.

"Hey," he said. "I didn't ask you to make me breakfast every day."

"Well, I'm not going to."

"Melissa."

She tossed some chopped tomatoes into the pan. After mixing them briskly, she poured in beaten eggs. More sizzling as the liquid hit the hot metal, then the pan quieted.

Melissa faced him. She held the wooden spoon in her hand. "I just don't want you to get the wrong idea."

"I'm not getting the wrong idea, Mel. You have an intense and demanding job. You're pregnant. And you think I'm going to make you cook and clean for me?"

He opened the fridge and reached in for the carton of orange juice. He gave it a quick shake and then poured himself a glass he'd pulled from the cupboard by the fridge.

Melissa still hadn't said anything.

He sipped, not even glancing at her. "I'll make you breakfast tomorrow," he said, unable to hide his annoyance. "Then we'll be even."

"Sorry," she said after a silence.

"Hey, it's no big deal. Better that we work these issues out right away."

"Kyle, look at me."

He did.

She blew out a stream of air. It lifted a strand of dark hair. "I guess I got up on the wrong side of the bed this morning."

He watched her for a moment, then told her in a soft voice, "You know, we will figure this out."

He said it with more confidence than he felt at

that particular moment. They had so much to deal with.

Like sex.

He wanted to sleep with her. To make love to her.

But she wasn't ready, and he didn't know if she would ever be. He didn't know if that one night they'd spent together was all he would ever get of her. He'd be damned, though, if he would let himself push her again the way he had with the television, or with that kiss at his apartment a week and a half ago.

That kiss.

That torturously mutual kiss. So much more genuine than the tepid one they'd shared during their church wedding yesterday.

He took a big gulp of his juice. He suddenly felt eager for Melissa to go off for her overnight shift.

ON SUNDAY MORNING Anita walked back into the bedroom she shared with Troy a couple of minutes after leaving it.

She'd planned to take a shower.

She'd also planned for this to be a relaxed morning together. Troy didn't have to work until twelve-thirty. They'd already stayed in bed for half an hour, lounging. As Melissa had said, taking a while to get out of bed helped the morning sickness.

But she hadn't counted on what she'd found when she went to use the bathroom.

Oh, God.

Troy eyed her over the top of the newspaper. "Anita, what's wrong?"

She heard her voice quiver. "I'm spotting," she said.

He put the paper aside. "Come here."

She sat on the bed next to him. He put his arms around her. She tried to breathe.

"It's okay," he said.

"I'm *bleeding.*"

"It just started?"

"Yes."

"How heavy is it?"

"I don't know. Not very. I can't really tell."

"Then let's see what our baby books say, and maybe call Dr. Porter."

"I'm afraid. Oh, Troy, I'm so afraid."

CHAPTER TEN

AFTER HER LONG SHIFT at the hospital Melissa came home to an empty house.

She was surprised by the way it felt. Different. As if she'd expected him to be there.

Or maybe it was just seeing the boxes stacked neatly in the hallway, waiting to be unpacked.

This whole business of being married was too strange. Even the weight of her wedding band... She felt as if someone had tied a brick to her finger. Eventually she would get used to it, but for now she was excruciatingly aware of it.

The door to Kyle's room stood open. Melissa looked in but didn't enter. He and Jerome had brought over a few plants, though not the ficus from his living room. Also his desk and some lamps. He hadn't hung anything on the walls yet. Neither, she noticed, had he returned the photo of Felicity and him to the top of the dresser.

But that didn't necessarily mean anything.

Kyle strolled up the front walk a few minutes later, sweaty. He had a basketball under his arm.

''Sorry,'' he said. ''Meant to be home when you got back. The game went on a little long.''

She watched him for a moment, reading his mood.

Nonchalant. Same old Kyle. Yesterday morning hadn't happened.

Fine.

"You win?" she asked.

He grinned. "That's what took a while. But yes."

"How's Jerome?"

"A little slow today. But he made every damned shot."

"Kyle… That's not what I meant."

"He's doing well. You want to have him over to dinner sometime?"

Inviting people over to dinner. That was what married couples did, wasn't it?

"Maybe in a few weeks. When we get settled."

Kyle opened the hall closet. He held the basketball in one hand. "Okay if I store this in here?"

She had a moment of wondering where on earth his stuff was going to go. "This is your house, too, Kyle. And you don't have to be here whenever I get home."

He put the basketball away, then shut the closet door. "We *are* married now."

She felt tense. "That doesn't mean we have to live in each other's pockets."

"I'm not trying to smother you, Melissa. But maybe since we're sharing a house we should at least try to leave each other notes."

She realized he was right. She was just picking a fight to avoid dealing with other emotions. Just as she had yesterday morning. "Okay. That's a good idea," she said, apologizing.

"We're used to being independent," Kyle said.

I'm used to not being in love. Not knowing how I feel about you.

"Yeah," she said.

God, this was so…disturbing. She'd told herself a hundred times in the past few weeks that the fear she felt wasn't rational. What was there to be so afraid of, except losing him? Yet it wasn't a fear she could merely dismiss, and in the past few weeks her low-lying, constant state of dread had intensified. She'd gone from two people to worry about—her father and Anita—to four—Kyle and the baby, as well.

It wasn't what she'd wanted.

She didn't like to form the kind of bonds with people that made her worry about their happiness and safety. Didn't like to have to think about the possibility of losing them.

"We can still be independent," Kyle said. "But maybe make a few concessions."

"It's just all the changes, Kyle." She stared at the floor. "I'm sorry I've been cranky."

"Don't worry about it. How was work?"

"Busy."

"You get any sleep?" he asked.

"Not much." She was glad they'd all decided

to cancel Sunday dinner at her father's house that night. She wouldn't have been up to it.

Kyle nodded toward her bedroom. "Why don't you grab a shower and take a nap."

"You first, I think."

He grinned, looking so much like the Kyle she'd known all these years. "What are you saying? That I stink?"

KYLE SPENT MONDAY morning clearing his desk. He and Melissa had a long-standing plan to spend the afternoon working together on the clinic's fall fund drive.

Before settling down to work they walked across Burnside Street into the wealthier area of downtown. They went to a French bakery and café that served sandwiches and salads. Healthy food for Melissa's pregnant body.

Walking back toward the clinic, they spotted Zita sitting in a doorway up ahead and stopped to talk.

Kyle said to Melissa, "This is the dog I was telling you about."

"Frank," said Zita.

"This is Frank," Kyle corrected. The Chihuahua nestled inside Zita's coat, with just his head protruding. Big wet eyes and long snout.

"He's cute," Melissa said.

"She," Zita said. "Frank's a she."

"She's cute, then." Melissa knelt and reached

out a hand. Frank sniffed it, then gave it a quick lick. "And sweet."

Zita scratched Frank's head. "She's my buddy."

"We've got to get to work, Zita," Kyle said. "See you around."

"I've never seen her so mellow," Melissa commented after they were halfway down the block.

"No kidding." It was an improvement even over the last time Kyle had seen the woman. "She really loves that dog."

MELISSA AND KYLE HAD a good afternoon together. They were getting along again. It was almost like old times, working in his office on the fund drive, she thought, just as they had in previous years.

She was almost annoyed when her pager went off.

Glancing down at the display, she recognized Anita's number. "It's my sister," she told Kyle.

Without asking—she didn't need to ask—she picked up the phone on his desk.

Anita answered and immediately started crying.

"Anita, what's wrong?"

It was a while before she could talk. When she finally did, her news was worse than Melissa had expected. "I'm losing my baby."

Melissa felt her stomach clench. Fear jolted her, bringing back all the reasons she'd been so terrified to find out she was pregnant. "Did you talk to Dr. Porter?"

"I just came back from her office."

Which meant it was probably true. "Oh, Anita."

"I've been spotting since yesterday morning."

"Honey, why didn't you call me sooner?"

"I—I didn't want to bother you and Kyle so soon after your wedding."

"We wouldn't have minded."

Anita sniffled. "Mel, I'm really freaked-out."

"I'm downtown," she said. "But I'll be there as soon as I can."

SHE FOUND ANITA in the bedroom, curled up under the covers. "Hey," she said. "Are you doing okay?"

Anita shook her head.

Melissa sat on the bed and gave her sister a hug. "Tell me what's been going on."

Her face tight with strain, Anita described the symptoms she'd been having. "Dr. Porter says there's nothing they can do about it, that we have to wait and see. I've barely been out of bed since yesterday morning. But I'm having cramps and the bleeding's gotten worse. I know I'm miscarrying."

It sounded as if she was, from everything Melissa knew.

"Are you in pain?"

"The cramping hurts like crazy. God. Oh, God. I knew this was going to happen."

Melissa didn't reply. Most of the things her sister worried about never came to pass. But every once in a while one of them did. She just wished it hadn't been *this* particular thing. "When does Troy get home?" she finally asked.

"After seven. He's been working a lot to earn money for the baby. I guess he won't need to do that anymore. Not if there is no baby." On the last sentence, Anita's voice cracked.

"It'll be okay," Melissa soothed. "You'll be able to get pregnant again."

"People die from miscarriages."

"We'll make sure that doesn't happen."

"I'm scared," Anita said.

Melissa took her sister's hand. She gave it a reassuring squeeze. "I know you are."

Anita yanked her hand away. "You don't know anything about being scared. You've never been scared in your life. Nothing touches you."

The lashing out was sudden, but not unexpected. Anita sometimes got this way under stress. Melissa let the words wash over her like rain sheeting off a roof. She needed to be strong for Anita. It was the least she could do to make up for everything else that was missing from Anita's life. To make up for the lack of a mother and a brother.

"I'm here for you," she said. The words came out even, calm, without a hint of the effort it took to say them.

A few moments passed.

"Sorry," Anita said.

"It's okay."

"HOW'S YOUR SISTER?" Kyle asked when she got home. He'd obviously been listening for her car, and opened the door before she had a chance to use her key.

"Not good." Melissa had left soon after Troy returned, and had driven home in a funk. "I told them to call if they needed anything. Even if it's the middle of the night. But I don't think they will."

"Is she definitely miscarrying?"

"Yeah."

"Oh, hell. I'm so sorry." He hugged her then, drawing her into his arms and letting her rest against him. Letting her lean into him. Melissa savored the moment. The closeness. The strength flowing from him.

It was nice not to have to be strong for him.

Nice to simply feel her own emotions, confused as they were. She permitted herself to shed the pain and concern of the past few hours, the tension she'd built up in her body. Tension that could not be good for her baby.

She allowed them just to be friends. The old way. *Let him comfort you,* she told herself. *He's strong. As strong as you are.*

Kyle held her for a long time.

When he released her he looked into her face, assessing her mood. His own face conveyed his regret for Anita and Troy. "Did you eat anything?"

She shook her head.

"Maybe food would help."

Melissa followed him into the kitchen. He'd made a pot of brown rice and had washed some vegetables for steaming.

Her doctor's voice tried to tell her miscarriage was just a natural process. Nature dealing with chromosomal abnormalities or a damaged fetus at an early stage. Preserving reproductive resources for future pregnancies by discarding nonviable tissue. Not even a death, really.

Her doctor's voice wasn't louder than the one that said this miscarriage was profoundly unfair. It was the death of a being Anita and Troy had already started to love.

And it wasn't louder than the awful voice that said, *Thank God it wasn't me*.

Kyle popped the vegetables into a steamer basket in a pan. "Is that one of the reasons you didn't tell me about your own pregnancy for so long? The possibility of a miscarriage?"

She took her hair out of its clasp, then ran her fingers through the strands. "Part of it," she admitted.

If she had miscarried, then life could have gone on just like before. Nothing would have changed except for the fact of their brief sexual interlude, and they could have gone on pretending that hadn't happened.

"There was also the general fear and awkwardness," she added.

"Fear?"

How could she even talk about the fear she felt? She'd spent most of her life keeping people at a distance so she wouldn't have to face the risk of losing them.

"Of giving birth to a child and then…someday losing him or her. It paralyzed me. I think sometimes I almost wished for a miscarriage."

It still did paralyze her sometimes, but she hid it. She had learned, a long time ago, that there were things you kept from other people. Secrets. Usually for their own happiness and sometimes for your own.

Kyle watched her, absorbing her confession. "Do you have regrets?"

More regrets than she could ever articulate.

"About wishing that?" she asked. "Or about having a viable pregnancy?"

"Either. Both."

"Yes to the first. No to the second. I'm scared about the future, but I can't regret it. You?"

"I don't regret your being pregnant. But it still isn't something either one of us would have planned."

"No."

If it had been up to us we wouldn't have had a child together. Wouldn't have gotten married.

You don't love me.

They were silent for a while. The small amount of water in the vegetable pan came to a boil quickly. The lid rocked gently as the steam sought escape.

Other thoughts.

Thank God it wasn't me.

Guilt assailed her again. This relief was familiar and painful. She'd felt it after the accident when she was eight years old. Back then it had cemented her sense of despair. That she could experience what she had and still be glad she'd been saved... It was unimaginable. There was no way to make up for it, no matter how she tried.

"Does your father know?" Kyle asked.

"Not yet. Anita wants to wait until it's over."

"Understandable, I guess. How do you think he's going to take it?"

Melissa took a breath. "Badly. But at least he won't have any unmarried pregnant daughters."

Her father would have been able to handle it if just Melissa had gotten pregnant, and if she hadn't married Kyle. He wouldn't have been happy. He wouldn't have understood. But he would have learned to live with it.

But it was too late to think about that. She and Kyle were married now. And it would still be better for the baby to have two parents at home. Two married parents.

One of whom had fallen in love with the other.

"I don't think that will be much of a consolation," Kyle said, continuing their conversation.

"Maybe Dad will be relieved. I don't know."

All she really knew tonight was that she was definitely attached to her baby. And that made the potential pain of losing her or him greater still.

She'd tried to avoid that kind of pain by avoiding love. And by avoiding children.

She'd blown it on both counts.

She loved her baby unconditionally. And she didn't know if she had the strength to lose anyone else.

MELISSA WANTED TO WASH UP after dinner. Kyle let her. There wasn't much for her to do anyway.

He went into his room and worked at his desk, filling out a stack of change-of-address cards he'd meant to send out last week. After a few minutes the sounds from the kitchen tapered off. Turning from his desk, he found Melissa leaning against the door frame. She had her arms crossed in front of her.

"What if we lose *our* baby?" she asked.

He'd read about miscarriage in their pregnancy books. "I thought the risks went down after the first trimester."

"Some do. But anything can happen. Fevers, accidents, infections. I could even have a stillbirth, or the baby could die within hours of being born."

He rolled his office chair toward her. "You've been thinking about this."

"Yes." Melissa came into his room. She perched on the edge of the bed.

He moved even closer, until their knees were nearly touching. "I worry about it, too." It was hard to let himself get attached knowing things could end badly. He already *was* attached. And it was easy to imagine things ending badly. That was how life worked, as he'd learned long ago.

"It could happen. Just because I haven't had an early miscarriage doesn't mean I'll carry this baby to term."

Every prospective parent must go through this, Kyle thought.

The worry.

One of their pregnancy books contained a section on things that could go wrong during a pregnancy. The authors warned readers not to look at the section unless they suspected a problem.

Who could read a warning like that and heed it? It was like Pandora being told not to open the box. So Kyle had read, and the possible complications of pregnancy had haunted him. There were risks not only for the baby but for the mother.

He'd had to remind himself that if he somehow lost Melissa and their baby it would be different from losing Felicity. It wouldn't be an intentional action on anyone's part, for one thing.

And he wasn't in love with Melissa.

Though that felt like a small comfort. He still liked her. Cared about her as a friend.

A sexy friend.

He put a hand on her knee. "Whatever happens," he said, "we'll get through it."

But of course there might not be much of a *we*. If they lost their baby they would have no reason to remain married. There would be no child to raise, no child who needed two parents at home to provide balance in his or her life. He and Melissa would revert to being just friends, not parents of the same child.

They would probably get an annulment. Go back to their separate lives and only see each other a few times a week, maybe fewer.

He would be free again.

Maybe they would drift apart.

The thought bothered him more than he wanted to admit.

MELISSA SLEPT BADLY that night. Horribly. She dreamed of traffic accidents, miscarriages, catastrophes in the E.R.

Anita's miscarriage was hitting her hard. The constant reminder. The slow, dragging loss. She felt guilty for still being pregnant. Wished she could do something to make it better, to make the pain go away.

But there was nothing she could do except be

strong for Anita. Just as when she was eight years old.

Be strong.

Even though she felt more shaken, more fearful, than at any time since her pregnancy had begun.

STARTING THE NEXT DAY, Melissa spent as much time as possible at Anita's. The bleeding and cramping continued.

"I can't believe this might last another week," Anita said. "I'm miserable."

The cramps clearly made her uncomfortable, but her self-castigation was even worse.

No matter what Melissa said, Anita wouldn't stop blaming herself for the miscarriage. Melissa showed Anita all her baby and pregnancy books, each of which said that early miscarriages just happened, that there was almost never an identifiable cause.

"Most women don't do a lot of oil painting," Anita insisted. "Most don't have anxiety attacks the way I do."

"Most women who have one early miscarriage go on to have a perfectly healthy baby the next time around."

Anita was stonily silent in response to this.

"Have you talked to Troy about trying again in a few months?"

"Yes."

"What did he say?"

"Look, I don't want to talk about it."

"I'm just trying to help," Melissa said.

"Well, we're having problems, okay? A lot of couples do."

WEDNESDAY AFTERNOON Kyle was facing down a grant proposal when Barbara rapped on the door frame. Melissa hadn't yet arrived for her shift, and he felt restless.

Inexplicably eager to see her.

"What's up, Barbara?"

She walked into his office. "Hi, Kyle."

She wanted something. It was that tone of voice. The fact that she'd bothered to greet him. He smiled. "I can see *right* through you, Nurse Ratched."

"Then just say yes."

He cocked his head. "Maybe."

"Good enough for me." Barbara turned to go.

"Uh-uh," Kyle said.

She stopped. Leaned against the doorway. "The kid needs somewhere to be. Something to do."

And they needed help at the clinic.

Barbara didn't have to say it. The problem was, sometimes the kids and adults who needed somewhere to be and something to do took as much time and energy to supervise as they saved in work time.

"Which kid?"

"Blue. You've met him. He's a smart one."

"I remember." Kyle thought back to his one meeting with the boy at the clinic, and the several times he'd seen him at Buddy's Café. He was a good worker. Probably worth the risk.

Especially when Kyle asked himself, *What if this were my kid?*

What if his own child ended up on the streets as a teenager for some reason? It was hard to imagine how that could happen, but at the same time it didn't take much to send a family into a financial hole. Or for serious disagreements to spring up between parents and children.

If this were his child, then he would want someone to extend a hand. To be a solid adult presence in the kid's life. Maybe give him something to aspire toward.

"How did all this come about?"

Barbara shrugged. "I ran into him on the street. We got to talking."

"Is this your idea?"

"His. So it's settled, then?"

Kyle peered at her. "Barbara, was saying no ever an option?"

"Nope."

Kyle glanced at the clock on his wall. "He must still be working at Buddy's."

"Yeah. He said he'd come over after his shift there. See if you could use him."

"We can't pay him."

"Hey, you can hardly pay me."

After Barbara left, Kyle went out front to talk to Whitney. "Can you use some extra help this afternoon?"

Whitney grinned at him. "I can *always* use extra help."

"Good. We've got a volunteer who might show up." He explained about Blue and suggested a couple of projects he might help with. "Send him back when he gets here. I want to talk to him first."

Melissa arrived a short while later. They hadn't interacted much the past few days. She'd been at work, then out at Anita's the night before. This morning he'd left the house while she was still in bed.

Up until recently he hadn't minded seeing her only a few times a week. Now he was getting used to having her around more.

Maybe getting *too* used to it.

She already had a clipboard in hand when she stepped into his office to say hello. "Anita says hi," she told him. "I just came from a quick visit."

"She's still uncomfortable?"

"Yeah. Emotionally as much as physically." She hesitated. Looked as if she had more to say but wasn't sure how it would be received.

"What is it?"

Melissa closed his office door and advanced farther into the room. Sat down on the chair in front of his desk. "She and Troy. They...aren't really getting along right now. She feels as if she needs some space from him. I...I said she could stay with us for a few days."

Kyle took a moment to digest her statement. And its implications.

"She's family," Melissa said.

"I know. And of course she's welcome to stay. But where?"

As if she couldn't help herself, Melissa leaned forward and straightened a stack of files on his desk. She picked up a loose paper clip and stuck it back on the magnetized dispenser. "Your bedroom."

"And I'll sleep where—on the couch?"

She shook her head.

CHAPTER ELEVEN

MELISSA DIDN'T MEET his gaze as she spoke. "No. I don't want my sister to think there's anything wrong with our marriage."

"So you're saying I should…sleep in your bed." Kyle felt an involuntary jolt of arousal at the thought. But sharing a bed didn't mean having sex. He'd be crazy to think it did.

"Yeah," she said.

He forced himself to sound calm. Mild. "This is a change."

"It's just for a couple of days." She stared down at the clipboard on her lap. "Anita assumed her old room was vacant. I couldn't have said no even if I'd wanted to."

"Because she's family."

"And we stick together."

Kyle clasped his hands on his desktop. "What about my stuff?"

His belongings were scattered all over the room. The place looked lived-in.

"She won't be over until eight or so. If we skip dinner with Barbara and Whitney tonight we can make it look as if the room's only a storage area."

He raised an eyebrow. "Or we could just come clean."

"I thought about that. I'd rather stick with our original agreement to keep the details of our marriage to ourselves. This wouldn't be a good time to tell her the truth. She's already got too much to deal with. I don't want to burden her."

"Okay, then."

"You'll go along with it?"

It's just for a couple of days. He could stand the torment that long, couldn't he? "If you think it's best."

"I do." She stood up to go.

At that moment a knock sounded at the office door.

"Come in," he called, rising, as well.

Blue opened the door.

"Hey, how are you?" Kyle said, walking over. "Melissa, this is Blue. He'll probably be helping us out on the administrative side. Blue, this is my wife, Melissa. She volunteers her medical services one afternoon a week."

My wife.

It still sounded strange on his lips. He hadn't said it to very many people.

My wife, whose bed I will actually share tonight.

A temporary situation.

Kyle cut his thoughts short.

As Melissa and Blue greeted each other, Kyle

focused on the changes that had taken place in the boy during the past few weeks.

Although Blue had started working at Buddy's only recently, it seemed to have helped him a lot. He wasn't so twitchy and furtive. He stood up straight and didn't seem embarrassed to be there.

Melissa held up her clipboard. "Gotta go. Nice meeting you, Blue."

Kyle waved Blue to a seat. "Barbara tells me you'd like to get involved."

"Yeah."

"Any particular reason?"

Blue shrugged. "I could use someplace to be. Something to do. This seems like a good place."

Kyle appreciated the honesty. He could understand that a warm spot on a rainy afternoon wasn't insignificant.

"We can't pay you," he said, returning the honesty. "I'd like to be able to, but there's no funding."

"That's okay."

"I'm sure you need money…"

"Yeah. But I've already got the job at Buddy's."

Kyle knew exactly how much that job earned. Meals and a few bucks a day. He said, "Sometimes our volunteers don't work out."

"I'm not going to steal stuff." Defensive. It was a glimpse of the boy from the first visit.

"I didn't think you would. All I'm saying is that

you'll need to work hard, even though you're a volunteer.''

''Sure.'' His equilibrium was back. ''And if I don't like it, I'll quit.''

Kyle watched the boy for a moment. Blue looked him in the eye, not shy. Kyle was impressed. ''I think we have a deal.''

He introduced Blue to Whitney and she got him set up with some filing that was long overdue.

MAKING THE SPARE ROOM LOOK as if Kyle used it as a closet and an office rather than a place to sleep was easy. Melissa changed the sheets and removed his books from the nightstand while he selected items of clothing from the closet and dresser. Sometime during the past few days the photo of him and Felicity had returned to the top of the dresser. A brief reappearance. He stashed it in one of the drawers, under a stack of T-shirts. Melissa pretended not to notice, but for a moment she actually hated Felicity. Hated her for her weakness in committing suicide, for hurting Kyle so badly and for preventing Kyle from being able to love *her.*

As soon as she had the thought she was ashamed. She had no right to hate a dead woman. Like everyone else, Felicity had just been doing the best she could.

And if Felicity had faced life and married Kyle, Melissa wouldn't have him now.

Still castigating herself, she took Kyle's books to her room and set them down by the bed.

The suddenly very *small* bed.

Her full-sized mattress had always seemed big enough for her. And it would probably be big enough for a blissfully married couple who didn't mind sleeping all tangled up with each other. But for her and Kyle…

"What's so fascinating?" he asked from directly behind her.

She whipped around, feeling herself flush. "The, uh, the bed."

Kyle nudged open the closet door and hung a handful of clothes next to hers. Then he came and stood beside her. They both stared down at the bed.

"It's not very big," she said.

"I think we're stuck with it. We don't have time to get the one in my apartment."

Kyle's old bed was queen sized, unlike the two that were here in the bungalow. Not *much* bigger, but enough to make a difference. Unfortunately he was right—they didn't have time.

"Hey," he said, "plenty of couples sleep in smaller beds than this all over the world."

Plenty of *couples,* she thought. They weren't exactly a couple, though, were they?

LATER, ALONE in her room, Melissa stared at the bed. Anita had already gone to sleep, physically

and emotionally exhausted. Kyle was still up, doing some paperwork in the living room.

It's okay, she told herself. *I can handle this.*

It was just Kyle. Her friend Kyle. And nothing
was going to happen. They were just pretending to
have a normal marriage. Sharing a bed so Anita
could have her old room for a few days.

She put on a nightgown. Simple and white, nothing to write home about. Nothing she wouldn't
wear to walk out on the front lawn to get the paper.

Well, not quite. But almost.

It was certainly nothing to send the wrong signals.

Melissa stood at the foot of the bed for a long
time, looking down at the mattress.

She'd put her water glass on the table on the
near side of the bed. The medical journal she'd
been reading last night was on the other one. Next
to Kyle's books.

It was time to choose a side of the bed. Right
or left. She didn't know whether it mattered, or
whether it would matter in the future—they would
share this bed for only a few nights this week—
but somehow the decision seemed momentous.

Because sleeping beside each other wasn't such
an accident this time. It was planned and he was
her husband now.

And she didn't know if she wanted to be on the
right-hand side of the bed or the left.

She heard Kyle's footsteps in the hallway and dove for the far side of the bed.

Way on the far side, with as much mattress as possible in the middle.

But it was just a false alarm. He didn't come in. She heard him walk past the door again, headed back toward the living room.

Her breathing slowed. She turned off the light and lay in the darkness. Her familiar mattress might as well have been a rough granite slab for all the comfort it gave her.

Minutes passed. She tossed and turned. She felt like a schoolgirl. Or a blushing bride waiting for her husband. But they weren't going to *do* anything. They were just making the illusion complete.

I'm definitely not ready to make love with him.

Finally she just gave up. She snapped on the light and grabbed her medical journal. Sitting up against the headboard, she found her place and began to read again.

From time to time she heard Kyle moving around the house. Quiet sounds. The water running in the kitchen, a door opening and closing.

After about half an hour Kyle slowly opened the door and walked into the bedroom.

"You're still awake," he murmured.

"Yeah."

"Did I keep you up?"

She shook her head. On an ordinary night, the

sounds he made would probably have been sooth-ing.

She looked at him. That strong jawline, slightly crooked nose. Forearms with their sprinkling of hair. Hands.

Relax, she told herself. This wasn't actually that unusual. After all, didn't a *lot* of married couples sleep in the same bed without making love?

He started to unbutton his shirt.

She didn't know where to look. Leaping to turn out the light seemed like an overreaction, as did trying to avoid seeing him. What could she do—stare at the curtains as if they suddenly held clues to the meaning of life?

So in the end she just watched him.

Six buttons on his shirt. He slipped it off his shoulders. Holding it by the collar, he shook it out to unroll the sleeves. He lifted the lid on her wicker laundry basket and dropped the shirt in.

"I'll do a load or two tomorrow," he said, in-clining his head toward the basket, keeping his voice low so he wouldn't disturb Anita.

"Okay."

His socks were next. Then he unbuckled his belt and slid it out from the loops. He hung the belt in their closet.

And then he unsnapped his jeans.

Her mouth felt dry. "You do, uh, wear…"

"Boxers to bed?" he finished for her. "Yes."

"Good."

He pushed the jeans down his legs and stepped out of them. After folding them, he put them on the shelf at the top of her closet.

The mattress dipped as he got into bed. He pulled the sheets up and rested on his back. "Good night, Melissa."

She reached for the lamp. The room went dark. Melissa turned onto her back and they lay there, the two of them, like horizontal statues. She was overwhelmed by the sound of her breathing, which seemed unnaturally loud in her ears. Slowly she brought it under control, made it quieter and deeper and more measured. And then she could hear his, just as slow and deep as hers, but definitely not the breathing of a sleeping man.

It didn't take a lot of bedroom experience to determine that.

She felt heat coming from his body. Sleeping near him was dangerous, if only for the purely physical fact that heat attracted on a cool fall night. Heat would draw her toward him.

This man.

Her husband.

Who'd made it clear all along that he wanted to make love with her again.

CHAPTER TWELVE

MELISSA FELT RESTLESS and turned on her side. The position left her facing Kyle across a foot of open space. It was more comfortable for her body, and more the way she would have to sleep later in her pregnancy, when lying on her back wouldn't be advisable.

Her eyes had gotten used to the dim light seeping through the white curtains at the window. In the city, nothing was ever completely dark except when the power went out. Between the streetlights and the glow of her alarm clock across the room she could make out his features.

His sculpted profile, in shadow tones. The strong nose and chin. Perfectly still.

She stared at him for a long time, watching the rise and fall of his chest. It had been hard to sleep sometimes, recently. Melissa hadn't known whether to put it down to the changes in her body due to her pregnancy or to the crazy events of the past few weeks.

Tonight, though, she could hardly blame her pregnancy. Her own confused feelings were causing her sleeplessness. She felt caught between two opposite desires.

One was to stay as far as she could from Kyle so she wouldn't get anymore entangled. The other was to forget about the consequences and scoot right over across the bed, into the warmth and comfort of his arms.

But those arms could provide only physical warmth and comfort, she reminded herself. Passionate friendship. Nothing more. Not love.

He was good at sex—very good—but he couldn't give her love. And she couldn't ask it of him. It was stupid even to think about it.

Felicity's picture.

In his dresser in the other room, under a stack of T-shirts.

Melissa felt the sudden urge to end this farce. To say, *Why don't you just go out to the couch? We'll tell Anita the truth in the morning.*

But she couldn't do that. She was the one who'd asked him to sleep in here. If she changed her mind, Kyle might get suspicious. He might begin to think there was a reason for her waffling, a reason for her courage to fail her.

A reason she couldn't let him discover.

She knew what Kyle was like. She'd seen how he was with women. How he was with the ones who got too serious, the ones who fell in love with him.

The most recent one, she remembered, had been

Alice. Beautiful, successful Alice, who'd made the mistake of getting too emotionally attached to Kyle during their brief, no-strings affair. Who'd become clingy and needy, and sent Kyle running for the nearest exit.

She wouldn't let that happen to her, Melissa vowed. Their child needed both of them in his or her life.

So she had to play it cool. Had to be her old calm and collected self.

"Melissa."

His voice. Husky and soft in the dark.

For a long moment she didn't say anything. Couldn't say anything. Her throat seemed to have constricted, to be incapable of speech.

Melissa, I know I said I wouldn't rush you. But I can't go another night without touching you.

And what would she do if he said that? Give in willingly? Grudgingly? Not give in at all?

"What?" she finally managed to say.

"You'll sleep better if you close your eyes." The words were warm, almost teasing. So very Kyle.

Melissa felt her skin grow hot. She closed her eyes. "How could you tell?"

Silence for a long moment.

"Your eyelashes on the pillow," he said.

She opened her eyes again. Blinked. Her lashes made a scraping sound against the fabric of the pillowcase. Surely she'd noticed that sound before, she told herself. But how long ago?

It wasn't the kind of thing that mattered when you slept alone.

And it probably wasn't the kind of thing that usually mattered when you slept with someone else. Except that this was different.

A real married couple wouldn't care about the sound of eyelashes on the pillowcase. They'd be much too busy with other things.

Like making love.

Or sleeping, damn it.

But if neither of them could sleep tonight…? If they both stayed awake until dawn, aware of each other but separated by the small amount of open bed?

Not good to think about.

Kyle turned onto his side, facing her. She could see his eyes as dark shadows in the deeper darkness. "Melissa, go to sleep."

"I'm trying."

"I know this is different for you. Difficult. It's different for me, too."

"Yeah."

"But I'm not going to attack you. I promise."

Which was what she wanted to hear, right? Or was it?

Melissa took a deep breath, then let it out slowly. She fell back on one of the techniques she used when she needed to sleep at the hospital but wasn't fully tired—on those rare occasions when that happened. She began counting backward from one thousand, trying to clear her mind of all extraneous thoughts.

She got most of the way to zero before falling asleep.

KYLE LAY IN BED next to Melissa for a long time before sleep claimed him. He listened to her breathing as she began to drift off. Eventually she fell asleep, and then her breathing was slow and even.

It did nothing to make his sleep come sooner.

Only the knowledge that they wouldn't have to share this tiny bed every single night soothed him. For another couple of nights he could deal with this. After that he would almost look forward to returning to the spare bedroom.

And then there was the other soothing thought. The thought that someday she would welcome him into her bed as a lover…

No, that thought didn't help.

He settled in for one of those frustrated, unfulfilled nights he'd known were inevitable when he'd agreed to this crazy marriage.

EARLY THE NEXT MORNING Melissa awoke as the dawn's light began to filter through the curtains into her bedroom. She felt content and impossibly well rested, considering how much trouble she'd had getting to sleep.

And considering the heavy arm draped over her torso, as well, she thought, blinking to full consciousness.

She'd left the windows open a crack for fresh air. Her curtains shifted slightly in the moving air.

Not unlike that morning in July…

She'd been aware of him the whole night long. Had known when he moved closer on the bed, had been fully aware of the fact that he'd spooned her and put his arm around her.

Of course she'd known she shouldn't let him. But it had been the middle of the night and her guard had been down. She hadn't had the strength to push him away. After all, she *loved* him. And when his arm was around her and his body was close to hers, convincing herself he might someday love her, as well, was all too easy.

Melissa turned her head gently and stared up at the ceiling. No exposed ductwork. No texturized cottage-cheese ceiling. Just an expanse of flat white paint glowing slightly orange with the dawn.

Her ceiling.

Her bed.

Kyle shifted. His arm pulled her more tightly against him. Heat throbbed into her from the length of his body. She felt it all the way from her toes to her scalp.

"Good morning," he said.

"Kyle?"

"Mmm?"

"We're going to need a bigger bed."

THEY ATE BREAKFAST with Anita that morning. Her cramping continued, and she was clearly depressed.

Melissa herself was still recovering from her night next to Kyle. The dangerous longings, the emotions she didn't want to feel.

The vulnerability.

In her work, she thought, she kept herself isolated from exactly this kind of situation. As a doctor she treated people in the emergency room and she either fixed them or failed to fix them. She got results, and fast ones. The short time frame didn't give her an opportunity to get attached, to become involved in the lives of her patients. To feel that crashing sense of loss when something didn't go right. After her intervention she was done, and it was so much easier that way.

But this was different.

A husband's arm around her. A husband's body next to hers.

Marriage.

A marriage, she realized, was all about time. Long chunks of it. Nothing temporary. Days and weeks and months and years all stacking up. The bonds of daily life bringing you more and more tightly together, enmeshing you, until losing your spouse made you feel as if a part of you had been ripped out, or as if someone had cleaved you down the middle without bothering to cauterize the wounds.

It was exactly what she hadn't wanted. But that was her life now....

She met Kyle at work that afternoon and went with him to shop for a new bed. King-sized. Initially he'd thought the purchase was a bit of an overreaction, but she'd made him see the necessity of it. They didn't just need the bed for the next few nights. In the future, when they had guests, they would have to share it, as well.

Unfortunately for Melissa, just walking into the mattress store was enough to give her shaky knees.

The showroom was a warehouse, an overwhelming jumble of beds and mattresses and box springs. Hectic signs in yellow-and-orange advertised this week's best deals. It looked as if there were hundreds of different kinds of mattresses for sale, from all the major brands.

A salesperson pounced on them. Sharp suit, slick hair. Smooth patter.

She felt herself start to panic.

"Kyle," she said. "I can't be here."

He led her out to the sidewalk. His focus, she noticed, was entirely on her. No apologetic grimace for the salesperson, no impatient sigh about his emotionally volatile pregnant wife.

"Are you okay?"

She nodded. "I am now."

"We'll go somewhere else."

He was her friend. Her Kyle. He understood her. *At least the part she let him understand. The part she didn't hide too deeply.*

"I know a place nearby," he said. "We should have gone there first."

It was far enough away to take the car, a showroom for handmade furniture in the 23rd Avenue shopping district. By some miracle they found a parking space right outside on the street.

She had to take a breath as they stepped through the door. The furniture was incredibly beautiful, all of it. Dressers, desks, chairs, mirrors. Her gaze roved the room and then latched onto a substantial mahogany sleigh bed.

"This place is going to be way too expensive," she said.

"They have some simpler things," Kyle said.

If they'd been a normal couple she wouldn't have hesitated to spend more money. Then this would have been the bed where they would sleep together for the rest of their lives.

Till death do us part...

The shaky feeling returned. It wasn't the orange-and-yellow cards, the jumble of mattresses, that had bothered her in the other place. It was the fact of a king-sized bed in her bedroom.

The fact of being married and in love with her husband.

Of being out of control.

She wanted to walk out, but she didn't. Couldn't. She had to face this.

Melissa ignored the sleigh bed. She loved it, but it was far too romantic for their situation. Instead she looked around the showroom until she found a handsome but unexceptional bed with a basic headboard. "How about this one?"

Kyle walked over. "Sure." He sat down on it. "Hard or soft?"

Mattress. "Medium," she said.

She wondered whether he would have let Felicity pick out such a simple bed.

He went to the counter and talked to a salesperson. Came back with a smile on his face. "We're in luck. They can deliver it this afternoon. I'll have to assemble it myself, though."

Tonight they could sleep in it together.

She hoped it would be less unsettling than sleeping in her tiny bed had been.

THE PHONE RANG THAT EVENING while Kyle was assembling the bed. Melissa answered it. There was a woman on the other end, asking for Kyle.

"Can I tell him who's calling?"

"Nina Carlton," the woman said in her melodic voice.

Melissa remembered Nina. She'd gone out with Kyle for a while a few years ago, until she'd been transferred to Atlanta. Nina was gorgeous, with jet-black hair and a tall, curvaceous body.

Ex-girlfriends calling her house.

She felt a twinge of jealousy, but reminded herself it was only to be expected, since her marriage to Kyle was so recent. And since it wasn't even a real marriage.

She gave the phone to Kyle and retreated to the living room where Anita was watching television. Anita was in a pretty bad mood. From the way she kept shifting on the couch, it was obvious the cramps were strong.

Kyle came out a few minutes later. "Can you help me in there for a second, Mel?"

Melissa followed him into the bedroom. He told her what he needed and she held the piece he indicated so he could fasten it to the footboard.

"How's Nina?" she asked, unable to squelch her curiosity.

"Good," Kyle answered. "She's in town for a few days. She invited us out for dinner tomorrow."

"Us?"

"Well, first she invited me. I told her I'd married you, so she invited both of us."

Melissa could imagine the woman's disappointment. Of course, she didn't know whether Nina was looking to rekindle anything with Kyle or just wanted to have a friendly meal.

"I should stay home with Anita," she told him.

"Okay."

"You can go if you want," she added reluctantly. It wouldn't be fair to make him stay home. She didn't want to be that kind of clingy, desperate wife.

As long as she remembers you're a married man.

THE FOLLOWING NIGHT, while Kyle was out at dinner with Nina Carlton, Melissa had a quiet evening at home with Anita. watching sitcoms and eating gingersnaps.

She wasn't able to pay much attention to the television. Friday night and here she was at home while her husband went out to dinner with a beautiful woman.

A beautiful woman he'd never really broken up with. Unlike many of his other girlfriends, who'd fallen in love with him, Nina had never lost her head. Their relationship had ended because of her promotion and forced move. Not because it had threatened Kyle.

Melissa knew her jealousy was irrational. Kyle may have claimed he couldn't be celibate for twenty years, but that didn't mean he would sleep with another woman only days after marrying her. Even if he didn't love her he wouldn't be that cold. Especially when they were sharing a bed.

Oh, she knew there were plenty of men, and women, too, who had affairs and then slept beside their spouses only a few hours later. But she didn't think Kyle would behave that way. He would feel too guilty and would have to say something to her.

In between shows Anita asked, "You're going to fix up my old room as a nursery, right?"

They actually hadn't made any plans to do so, but Melissa realized people would expect them to. She'd been thinking the baby might stay in her room until the summer, when they could add another room onto the house.

"I'm thinking of painting it," she said, even though the idea had never crossed her mind before that instant.

If she and Kyle painted it and started decorating it as a child's room, then he would stay in her bedroom.

Forever.

Which made Melissa feel very warm inside.

Letting him stay on would be an admission that she would someday be willing to have a sexual relationship with him. An ongoing sexual relationship.

Better with me than with someone else, she thought.

She didn't want to make love with him unless he loved her back, but she didn't see how she would get that option.

They watched another program, choosing a nature show about dolphins over an *X-Files* rerun. Anita went to bed halfway through. Melissa stayed up, waiting for Kyle.

He came home shortly before ten. Looking perfectly normal. He joined her on the couch.

She refused to ask whether anything romantic had happened between Nina and him. She wouldn't allow her insecurities to take over that much.

BY SATURDAY Anita's bleeding had stopped and she'd seen Dr. Porter. As well, Melissa had overheard Anita talking to Troy on the phone; it was clear she no longer felt such a need for space. Melissa could also tell that staying with her hadn't been quite what Anita had expected. Staying with your sister and her husband wasn't the same as staying with just your sister.

While Melissa was working at the hospital, Anita moved back to her apartment. She and Troy planned to go to her father's house earlier than usual for Sunday dinner so they could tell him about the miscarriage.

Melissa and Kyle came over at the usual time. Anita opened the door for them.

"How are you doing?" Melissa asked.

"Okay, I guess." Anita shrugged. "I still feel like crap physically."

"How did Dad take it?"

"Not great."

Melissa waited, but her sister didn't want to say more. She tried to imagine how the conversation had gone between the three of them and couldn't.

She didn't even know how *she* would handle it if she ever got into a similar situation.

She wondered whether Anita had tried to be gentle with their father or whether she'd put her own feelings first.

She heard the noise of water running in the kitchen.

"I'll go say hi," she said.

Anita retreated to the living room. Kyle went to speak with Troy.

She walked into the kitchen alone. Her father stood at the stove, cooking tomato sauce. The smell of herbs, grown in his garden and in the greenhouse attached to the back of the house, filled the kitchen.

"Hey, Dad."

He turned to her. He looked tired.

Old, suddenly.

It wasn't a physical change, she knew. His hair was the same distinguished gray it had been for years. The lines on his face had not deepened in the past week. But her perception had shifted. He looked not just like her father, growing older, but like an old man who was her father.

How many years did they have left? she wondered. Twenty, maybe, but men his age came into the E.R. all the time—

She stopped herself. Not helpful thoughts. Just another residual effect of Anita's miscarriage.

"How are you doing?" she asked him.

"Fine," he said, as she'd known he would. "How are you?"

"Good," she said, reassuring him. With Anita's miscarriage on his mind he would want to know that she wasn't going to miscarry, too. "I'm gaining weight just as I should be."

He nodded. His mouth was closed, a little tight around the edges. "I'm glad." He paused. "Your sister told me what happened to her baby."

Melissa went to the sink and rinsed out two empty tomato cans she found there. "It's been hard on her."

"It's very sad," he said.

"Yeah. We're all having a hard time with it."

Her father turned to stir his sauce. "Two little babies at the same time. It would have been exciting."

Melissa allowed herself a moment to picture her father with a baby on each knee. It would have made him very happy.

"These things happen. She'll be able to get pregnant again."

"I know. You want to help me cut some vegetables?"

"Sure." Melissa washed her hands and then went over to the counter where her father had laid out carrots, a red bell pepper and a cucumber. She selected a short knife from the drawer and began slicing the pepper.

Her father's house was comfortable to her. It

was the house she'd grown up in, the house they'd all shared with her mother and brother. Not much had changed in the twenty-three years since the accident. Most of the furniture was the same. Her father still used the same pots and pans. Still kept the knives in the same drawer.

She arranged the pepper slices on a plate, then reached for the cucumber.

Her father spoke. "You know, you don't have to hide these things from me."

Melissa studied him. His voice was calm. A little sad. "We thought..."

"I understand," he said. "It's hard news for all of us. Maybe it's better she didn't tell me right away. I don't know."

"I don't know, either."

Dinner was subdued. They sat around the dining-room table, five of them, and struggled to keep a conversation going. The sadness they all felt hung like smoke over the table. Anita seemed depressed. Troy, always quiet, was more withdrawn than usual. Her father seemed to want to focus only on his food.

Normally they all had a pretty good time together, but tonight reminded Melissa of the way things had been after the accident. Sometimes it had seemed that three unrelated people—instead of a family—were sharing a house.

MELISSA STEPPED OUT of her father's house into the cool October night. She drew in a breath of clean air and let it fill her lungs.

Light from the open doorway spilled out onto the lawn. Her shadow stretched long and thin against the grass.

Kyle joined her. "Ready?"

Definitely.

She wanted to go home to her little bungalow and be with Kyle. Just Kyle.

Anita was gone and they had the whole house to themselves. Melissa didn't want him to move back into the spare room. Anita's visit wasn't the only reason to have him share the bed. She'd been fooling herself to think so. Because she could have given her sister a place to stay without inviting Kyle into her bedroom. But she hadn't been able to resist the opportunity. The excuse. The ready rationalization.

On the drive home they talked about their plans to purchase the house. Kyle had scheduled an appointment with a loan officer at the bank. Melissa had called her landlord to confirm that he was still interested in selling.

At the bungalow she unlocked the door and pushed it open. She stepped in and held the door for him to walk through.

He came in. Brushed past her, slowly. Looking down at her.

She caught her breath. Time stood still. Did he do that kind of thing on purpose, or was it just her own awareness of him that made his every action so…interesting?

I love him.

The storm screen swung shut behind him, latching with its usual rattle. She closed the front door. Turned the lock in the center of the doorknob, threw the bolt.

Kyle stood in front of the hall closet, removing his leather jacket.

Melissa stared briefly at the breadth of his shoulders, his easy movements.

"I need a glass of water," she said. "Do you want anything?"

He shook his head.

She slipped into the kitchen and poured herself a small glass. It was late at night to be drinking fluids, considering how often her pregnant body felt the need to urinate, but she'd always believed in adequate hydration. Especially in challenging times.

Kyle sat on the living-room couch when she came back in with her glass. He leaned forward with his elbows on his knees.

Watching her.

"So," she said. "Tonight."

"Tonight."

The tension was palpable.

"Our bed."

"Is very comfortable," he said.

"About our...arrangement." She didn't know what to say, how to finish the thought.

"Yes?"

"I..."

He smiled at her. That charming, easygoing smile. "I understand," he said. "It was just temporary."

No, she wanted to say. That wasn't what she'd meant. *Come share my bed. If I'm going to risk losing you, I want as much of you as I can have.*

But her courage failed her. She couldn't be so outspoken, not when their feelings for each other were so lopsided. The best she could do was to ask, "Are there clean sheets?"

Hoping that there wouldn't be and she could say, *Oh, well. Another night together can't hurt.*

"I washed some this morning."

Melissa felt her mood sink. "Do you want help making the bed?"

"I already did it."

Had he been looking forward to moving back across the hall, counting the minutes until Anita left?

"You didn't have to do that," she said. It was feeble.

Kyle shrugged. "Not a big deal."

They watched an hour of television together that night, and Melissa sat closer to him than she had in the past. But when they got ready for bed, Kyle disappeared into his own room.

CHAPTER THIRTEEN

November

WHEN KYLE WALKED into the house one night a few weeks later, Melissa was just getting off the phone.

"That was our landlord," she told him. "Or should I say, the soon-to-be former owner."

"Oh, yeah?" Kyle asked, smiling. "You made a deal?"

"Yup."

"How much?"

She told him the figure.

He whistled. "You drive a hard bargain, Mel."

Their landlord had been glad to avoid the hassle of listing the property and working with real-estate agents. Not to mention not having to pay the commission. Even so, Melissa had negotiated a better price than Kyle had expected.

He took a moment to look around at the house they'd agreed to buy. The cozy living room and kitchen, the two bedrooms with their closed doors.

They'd settled back into a routine after Anita had returned to her apartment. With their separate bedrooms they were more and more like room-mates. To be friends was fine, but if they were sexless friends, living across the hall from each other... He still didn't want to be celibate for the next twenty years. But getting together with some-one else—that would get weird. Fast.

And he wasn't even sure he would want to. When he'd gone out with Nina last month he hadn't even felt tempted.

With Melissa, on the other hand, he felt the pull of temptation all the time. And he was damned sure he wouldn't get bored with making love to her.

Maybe it was time to push. Just a little. Because sleeping in the same bed had been a hell of a lot more interesting than sleeping separately, even if they hadn't made love. And as long as they were stuck with each other they might as well keep things interesting.

"When do we close on the house?" he asked.

"Three weeks." She told him the date. It was in early December.

A mortgage together. Both their names on the papers. One more thing locking them together. For some reason it felt just as big as getting married.

He said, "We can start making plans for an ad-dition on the back of the house."

"Yes. I've been thinking about where it should go. It'll mean giving up some garden space, of course."

Kyle paused, thoughtful. "But you know," he said, "the last thing we're going to want this summer is all the noise and hassle of a construction project when we have a brand-new baby."

"Oh. You're right. I hadn't thought of it that way."

"We could put it off for a year or two."

"Which would mean...?"

"Making my room into the nursery."

He watched her as he said it, and didn't miss the faint blush that rose into her cheeks.

"Okay," she said.

Just like that. Okay. So maybe she wasn't so resistant after all. At least to the idea of sharing a bed. Making love was probably still out of the question.

"We can shop for baby furniture soon," he suggested.

Melissa went to the couch and adjusted one of the cushions. She picked a speck of lint off the lamp shade. "We could paint the baby's room, too."

"Oh, what color?"

"Pale yellow, maybe."

Kyle smiled. "With the money you saved us on the house we could do the room in gold leaf."

"Regular paint is fine," Melissa said. "So how do you feel about yellow?"

"Hmm. What about pink if it's a girl and blue if it's a boy?

"Uh-uh. No way."

"I didn't think so."

"And anyhow, I don't think we should wait long. I think we should do it soon."

Soon. He had no argument with soon.

"Before your lease is up," she continued, "so we can spend a couple of nights at your apartment while the paint dries."

"So the fumes don't kill the ficus."

She smiled and nodded.

Pretty much all that was left at his apartment was the bed, the couch and the tree.

"Speaking of fumes," he said, "you probably shouldn't be painting anything. Just to be on the safe side."

Anita's miscarriage was too recent for them to ignore.

"That means you'll have to do it all. Though," she added, "we do have the money to pay someone, if you want."

He shook his head. "I like the idea of doing it myself."

She looked thoughtful for a minute. "What if you got someone to help?"

"You have someone in mind?"

"How about that guy—Blue? He's still volunteering at the clinic, right?"

Blue. Kyle had to think about that for a minute. He did a decent job at the clinic. He could probably paint a wall as well as the next person.

Still. Kyle had always made it a practice to keep his work and his home life separate.

"I'm not suggesting you adopt him, Kyle."

Suddenly tense. She got like this sometimes. A little moody, difficult.

He blamed it on the pregnancy and didn't pay much attention.

"Or what if we could get a whole bunch of people to help," he suggested. "See if some of our friends want to pitch in this Saturday. Paint in exchange for lunch, or something like that."

"Could you get it done in one day?" Her tension was gone.

"If we clean the walls and patched all the holes beforehand there's no reason we can't get two coats on in a day. And break for a lengthy lunch. And maybe go out to a movie."

"If it's Saturday then I'll be at the hospital that night. You'd have to stay at your apartment alone."

"I've done it before."

"And I'll join you there on Sunday night."

"Sounds good," he said. "Let me make some calls."

THEY WENT OUT for Indian food that evening. The restaurant was in a small commercial area not far from the house. Since it was a nice night, slightly cool, they walked there and back.

Strolling and talking, like friends.

Friends and something more, Melissa thought on the return trip, her belly full of saffron-scented rice and a mild spinach-and-potato dish.

Friends whose relationship was getting more and more intimate.

"So," she said, "I guess we're agreeing to share the bedroom for a few years."

"It seems that way."

Twenty years, maybe. And it was inescapable that they would make love at some point during that time.

But not tonight.

She had missed his presence these past weeks, more than she wanted to admit to herself. His warmth. His scent.

She just hoped he didn't bring the photo of Felicity with him.

SHE CALLED ANITA the next morning to see if she wanted to help with the painting.

Her sister answered the phone on the fourth ring, out of breath. As they said hello, Melissa could hear water running in the background.

Since Anita had moved in with Troy again they hadn't been seeing as much of each other. Anita had pulled back, away from her.

The couple of times she'd gone over to the apartment Anita had been depressed and unhappy. She hadn't seemed at all interested in talking to

Melissa. Had, in fact, seemed almost eager to get rid of her.

Melissa had respected that. Sometimes a person wanted to grieve in private. But she also wanted to give her sister support, give her handholds so she could pull herself out of her despair if she wanted to.

"Were you painting?"

"Yeah. Hang on a sec."

She put the phone down. Melissa heard splashing, then the water going off. "Sorry," Anita said. "I had to wash my hands. So what's up?"

"Just calling to see how you're doing."

"I'm fine."

It was a pretty noncommittal answer. Definitely an I-don't-want-to-talk-about-it kind of fine.

She explained about the painting party. "I thought you might want to come over and hang out. The painting shouldn't take long, and we'll have fun eating and going to a movie. Troy still works Saturdays, right?"

"Yeah, he does."

"Do you want to come?"

"I don't know, Mel. Maybe."

"Call me later in the week, then."

"Sure."

"I want to see what you've been painting recently," Melissa said. She had always liked her sister's artistic sensibility. Maybe art would give her a way out of her depression.

"There's nothing much to see," Anita said. "I don't have a lot to show for the past couple of weeks."

Another dodge. Anita was rarely reluctant to show her work. "How's Troy?"

Anita shrugged down the telephone line. "He's all right."

Melissa gave up. She stared out the window into her barren backyard. "Call me, okay?"

KYLE RAN INTO ZITA on the sidewalk outside the clinic the next afternoon.

"Goddamn rules and regulations," she snapped in response to his casual greeting. She was already well into their conversation. Well ahead of Kyle.

He raised an eyebrow, waiting. "How's the blood pressure? You still taking your pills?"

Zita grunted. "Fine, whatever."

She stared off for a moment. Kyle hadn't seen her like this for a long time. "What's up?"

"They're kicking me out."

"Who is?"

"Services."

Many of the single-room-occupancy hotels in Old Town were run by a city government agency called Old Town Services. Like other public agencies, they could be both positive and negative. If Zita really had a problem with them, it wouldn't be the first time that had happened between a resident and the agency.

"Kicking you out?" he asked. "Evicting you from your room?"

"Yeah."

"Why?"

Zita raised her voice. "Because they're a bunch of jerks, that's why!"

There were a few people on the other side of the street. A couple of women, smoking, and a middle-aged man in an ill-fitting suit, waiting for a bus. Only the middle-aged man turned to look at them. The women lived in Old Town. They knew Zita.

"What exactly happened?" Housing advocacy was not Kyle's territory, but he liked Zita despite her cranky ways, and it was possible she was misinterpreting the situation. They might all save a lot of trouble by sorting out the issue right here.

"Sent me a letter. Says I have to move out."

Kyle furrowed his brows. This was unusual. "Did they say why?"

"Bunch of jerks."

"Did they give a reason, Zita?"

"This time the mayor's going to *have* to talk to me," Zita muttered.

Kyle just watched her, waiting for her to focus on him again. As a recovering addict, Zita's health was fairly tenuous. He didn't want this incident, whatever it was, to set her back or even cause her a relapse.

"Have you got the letter with you?"

The woman dug into her pockets and came out with a folded piece of paper, crumpled and stained. She handed it over, still crumpled.

Kyle unfolded it, making an effort not to tear the already damaged paper. He skimmed it.

Frank, evidently, was the problem.

He met Zita's eyes. ''You know, this doesn't say you have to leave.''

Zita's mouth tightened, her lips thinning. ''Damned well does,'' she said after a pause.

''It says you can't keep animals in the hotel.''

''Same difference.''

He'd known the minute he read the letter that it would come to this. But he still had to try. ''You could find Frank another home.''

A shake of the head.

Several homeless residents of Old Town had dogs and cats. Unfortunately bonding with an animal pretty much meant that a person had to forgo the basic support systems of a low-income life. Single-room-occupancy hotels, shelters, soup kitchens.

''So you're going to move out?''

Zita cursed. ''I've been sneaking her in and out in my bag. She doesn't even bark.''

''Where are you going to go?''

Zita jerked her head toward the hills to the west. ''The park.''

''It's November.''

''No kidding.''

"I could take care of Frank," Kyle offered. "Bring her in to work every day so you could see her." He said it without considering any of the logistics, the health codes, the practicalities.

"She wouldn't hurt anyone," Zita said. "We're buddies."

"Is that a yes or a no?"

"No. Damn it. You're no help at all."

ANITA CALLED Wednesday night during *X-Files.*

"What time did you say that thing was on Saturday?"

"Late morning," Melissa said. "Ten-thirty, maybe. We can hang out in the kitchen if you decide you don't want to paint walls."

"Okay."

"I'm looking forward to it," Melissa said.

"Mmm. Me, too." But Anita didn't sound very enthusiastic. "Listen, I've got to go."

"Say hi to Troy for me."

"Sure."

Melissa felt oddly glad to put down the phone.

They were sisters. This wasn't the first time things had been difficult between them.

But it shouldn't have to be now. And she wished Anita wouldn't try to push her away.

WHILE MELISSA WAS at the hospital the next night, Kyle and Blue prepared the baby's room for painting. Kyle had debated whether or not to have Blue help, but had finally realized it wouldn't really hurt anything, and he could give the kid a decent wage for his hours of work.

They removed the furniture, then sanded down rough spots and started washing down the walls.

Blue was a good worker. Thorough and detail oriented, just as he was at the clinic. As they scrubbed, Kyle realized how little he knew about the kid.

He tried to open up a conversation, asking where Blue came from.

"Missoula."

"Why'd you leave?"

"I got a few too many broken bones."

Kyle let the subject lie low for a moment. "Hand me that bucket, would you? And that towel?"

He scrubbed at a smudge on the wall, then wiped the surface clean with the towel. "I can't tell if it's gone."

Blue looked closely at the wall. "It's gone."

"Did you have a lot of accidents, or was someone breaking them for you?" Kyle asked. The injuries might have been from skateboarding or some other sport, but that wasn't usually a reason to leave town.

"My stepfather."

"I'm sorry to hear that."

Of all the things Kyle and Melissa had experienced in their childhoods, physical abuse wasn't one of them. Unfortunately it had damaged the lives of many of the people who ended up on the streets.

"How long since you've been in school?" Kyle asked a while later.

Blue shrugged as he wiped a piece of trim around the open window. Outside, the side yard was dark. "Since last winter."

"You want to go back?"

"Don't care one way or the other."

At least that wasn't an outright no, Kyle thought. He knew some homeless kids in Portland went to school, although he didn't know how they did it. Schools, like a lot of other things, were set up for kids from families. Little things like parental permission slips got difficult if you didn't live with your parents.

Kyle went back to scrubbing.

Soon they moved on to patching holes—mostly small ones from hanging up photos and prints, but there were a few deep scratches left over from the previous tenants.

Luckily the walls had been off-white. It wouldn't be hard to cover them in the pale yellow. The job wouldn't require more than two coats.

They knocked off at nine, done for the night. Kyle drove Blue back to the shelter. They talked about basketball most of the way, discussing favorite players on Portland's hometown team, the Blazers.

Guy talk, Kyle thought. They'd talked about significant things for a while. They'd strayed close to their feelings, and told a little bit of the truth. Now they were just shooting the breeze.

He wondered what it was like to be so young and alone and far from home. Even if your home wasn't safe.

He'd once thought of leaving home, when he was about Blue's age, but the thought hadn't lasted long. He'd been having a hard time getting along with Craig and his mother, for reasons he couldn't remember, and he'd gotten it into his head to look for his father.

The plan had seemed good, until he remembered that his father wanted nothing to do with him. And probably wouldn't be overjoyed to have a sixteen-year-old kid show up on his doorstep. Wherever that was.

Staying home hadn't seemed like such a bad idea after that.

SATURDAY MORNING a group of their friends assembled at the house. Whitney had come over from the college. Jerome was there, and Blue.

Anita, Melissa noticed, was late.

Whitney and Blue knew each other, of course, but neither knew Jerome. Kyle introduced everyone. Moments later Whitney, always gregarious, was probing Jerome about his background and what he did for a living.

Melissa made coffee, herbal tea and multigrain muffins. She brought them into the living room. They all sat and talked for a few minutes before getting down to work. She noticed that Blue hung back from the others, as if unsure of his place. But Jerome asked him if he followed any sports teams and he perked right up.

Kyle checked his watch. "Okay, time to get cracking if we're going to make that movie," he said. They'd agreed to see the midday matinee of a new thriller while the paint dried, then come back for a big late lunch.

Melissa planned to spend the morning in the kitchen, making a salad to go with the pizza they would order that afternoon and catching up on her medical-journal reading.

She followed them into the now-bare nursery. Kyle opened the window and set up the box fan. He pulled out the cans of pale-yellow paint and handed out brushes and rollers. The tarps were already down to protect the floor.

"Time for you to leave," Kyle said.

"I'll send Anita in when she gets here," Melissa said.

She went into the kitchen and washed lettuce.

She sliced vegetables.

She made a balsamic vinaigrette in a jar.

Anita didn't show up.

Finally Melissa called her, just to confirm that she'd been blown off. And to make sure Anita was okay. Something might have happened to keep her at home.

Nothing had happened. "Oh, hi," Anita said when she picked up the phone. "I just didn't really feel like dropping over."

"You could have phoned."

"Didn't think of it. Talk to you soon, okay?"

Melissa stared at the phone for a second after hanging it up.

"Who was that?" Kyle asked.

"Anita."

"We finished the first coat."

Still preoccupied by her phone call, Melissa glanced at the clock on the stove. "It's only been forty-five minutes."

"That's quite a group of workers we assembled. Come see."

Melissa followed him to the baby's room. It looked just the way she'd expected. No, better than she'd expected. The pale-yellow color made the room seem much brighter and more inviting. Even with the painting cloths on the floor it looked wonderful.

"You guys are amazing," she said.

"Got any other rooms that need painting?" Jerome asked.

"Right across the hall," she said, smiling. "But we don't have the paint for it."

"And it's not prepped," Blue added.

Whitney grinned. "This was kind of fun. But

what I want to know is whether you have any more of those muffins.''

They put the paint away and went out into the living room.

"What time is the movie?" she asked Kyle.

"It's in an hour. And there I was, thinking we'd have to scramble to make it."

"Let's eat some more muffins, then," Melissa suggested. To Kyle she said, "I'm going to beg off the movie."

"Why? Aren't you feeling well?" There was instant concern in his eyes. "The fumes didn't reach the kitchen, did they?"

"No, it was fine." In fact, the room itself didn't even smell that bad. "That's not it. I've got to go talk to my sister. We need to straighten out things between us."

CHAPTER FOURTEEN

WHEN THE OTHERS LEFT for the short drive to the movie theater, Melissa got into her car and headed to Anita's apartment. She didn't bother to call first. Another brush-off was not what she needed.

And if Anita wasn't there, she would just turn around and head back home.

She rang the doorbell.

It was a while before Anita came to the door. Melissa heard the cover of the peephole being moved out of the way and knew her sister wouldn't leave her out there on the stoop like a door-to-door salesperson.

Anita turned the bolt and opened the door. She was dressed in her paint-smudged work smock and her hands were dirty.

"Hi," she said, obviously wary.

"Can I come in?"

Anita shrugged. The gesture seemed to say, *You might as well, since you're here.*

Not Anita at her most gracious.

Melissa walked in. The house was messy, but it had been for several weeks. Through an open door she saw Anita's art room. The lights were on and there was a canvas on an easel. Even from a distance Melissa could make out the shape of a pregnant woman.

She walked closer. From the doorway she could see that the floor was littered with charcoal sketches on sheets of newsprint.

"Don't look at those," Anita said. "They're just junk."

They weren't junk. Melissa could tell that at a glance. And she didn't stop looking. The sketches were obviously done with speed, and from both memory and imagination.

The subjects were varied.

Childbirth, pregnancy, miscarriage. A woman with a baby.

Herself.

An image of a woman, man and child in front of a simple house. The kind of image a child drew, except without Anita's skill.

And without a disturbing quality of anger running through it all.

"We need to talk," Melissa said.

"The sketches don't mean anything," Anita rushed to say. "They—I—"

The sketches meant something.

Be stronger than that, Anita, she wanted to tell her. *Own up to what you're doing.*

Anita started to gather them up, making a loose stack of the large newsprint sheets. Melissa felt suddenly tired. She didn't want to deal with this, and wondered whether she had the strength.

Always the strong one, Melissa.

"They're good," she said aloud.

"Yeah." Sarcastic.

"I didn't say I liked them. But they're good. They're very expressive."

"Now you know."

"What do I know?"

"How much I resent you."

Melissa waited.

Anita tossed the sketches down. "Oh, crap."

"It's okay," Melissa said.

Her sister rounded on her. "No, it is not okay. You're my sister and I'm being a total bitch to you."

"So be a bitch," Melissa returned. "I can take it."

Anita threw up her hands. "That's just it. *You can handle it. It's okay. Everything will turn out all right.* Nothing hurts you and nothing gets to you and you're so damned *perfect.*"

"Anita," she began, but Anita cut her off.

"I know I'm being childish and immature. But everything goes your way. You don't know what it's like to have things be difficult." She brushed a chunk of hair back from her face, the movement as intense as her expression. "Christ, you're probably even going to give birth without anesthesia, while I couldn't even get through a lousy miscarriage without screaming.''

"It's okay," she said automatically.

"And I'm sure your baby will be the most perfect and beautiful baby I've ever seen.''

While mine didn't even make it past three months. While mine wasn't viable.

Wasn't viable. What a phrase. Right out of a medical text, and it said nothing about the pain and the loss.

Anita went past her, out of the living room and into the kitchen. Melissa gave her a slow count of ten to calm down, then went after her.

She found Anita standing at the kitchen sink, staring out the window that overlooked the parking lot.

"I'm jealous, okay?" Anita said it without turning around. "I always have been.''

"It's okay," Melissa heard herself say.

Anita gripped the edge of the countertop by the sink. Her knuckles turned white. "No, it isn't.''

"May I have a glass of water?''

"What?" Momentarily startled. Then recovering. "Oh, sure." Anita reached into a cupboard for a glass from her mismatched set. She filled it with water and added some ice cubes.

Melissa took it. Sipped. She thought about the photo of Felicity in Kyle's drawer.

She said, "Maybe my life looks perfect on the outside, but it's not.''

"Don't bullshit me, Mel."

She didn't want any bullshit. And if getting rid of the half-truths could give her a good relationship with her sister, it was worth it. She knew Kyle wouldn't care if she told Anita about their marriage of convenience. He'd brought up the possibility himself last month.

Melissa took a deep breath, tried to speak and faltered. Swallowed and tried again. "Kyle doesn't love me."

"He worships the ground you walk on."

The response was quick. Calling her statement a lie. Anita hadn't even heard her, not really. And the assertion was false, too. It had no basis in reality, and wasn't meant to.

"We don't have sex. We haven't had sex since the night I got pregnant. Our marriage isn't what you think it is."

You could tell your sister things you wouldn't tell another living soul. Even if your sister hated you.

"It's an arrangement," she clarified. "For the baby's sake. For Dad's."

"You're friends," her sister said. "You get along well."

"Yes," Melissa said after a long hesitation.

Comprehension. "You're in love with him."

"Yes."

And why should that feel like a guilty confession? Like a secret she'd been harboring too long, something only she knew? She was married to the man, raising their child. Everyone would naturally assume she loved him. And yet the truth was a dirty little secret.

They were silent for a long time. Watching each other. Sisters.

"I want your support, Anita." No, that wasn't strong enough. "I need your support."

In an odd way, asking for it felt as good as getting it. She'd never asked for support before, not from Anita.

"Okay," Anita said, and it sounded like a promise.

"I'm not perfect."

"I know."

Melissa swallowed past a lump in her throat. "I lost the same mother you did. The same brother."

Silence. Anita's face was still. Inside, the pieces of a long-ignored puzzle were falling into place.

"Oh, damn," she said. She stepped forward and put her arms around Melissa. "Damn, damn, damn."

Melissa felt her body slowly relax as Anita hugged her tightly. The comfort was a long time coming, but not too late.

"Why didn't you ever cry?" Anita asked. Confusion, not anger, tinged her words. "Why didn't you ever break down? Why were you so damned strong, like it didn't touch you?"

"I cried," she said. "But not in front of you."

"Why not? We were a family. We were all we had left."

"Because I couldn't." And it was the same reason she wasn't crying now, the same reason her sister's comfort didn't reach all the way inside. A reason she could never tell. "Because I couldn't," she repeated

Anita seemed to sense that this was the limit of what Melissa could tell her. She held her more tightly. "You were always so strong."

"I know."

"And I hated you for it sometimes. Even when I depended on it."

"It's okay," Melissa said.

Hearing her say those familiar words, Anita half laughed, then hiccuped, then began to cry. "Oh, hell," she said. "It's happening again."

"No," Melissa said. "It's not."

And that was all she needed to say.

"DID I TELL YOU that Zita has moved out of her room?" Kyle asked as they all ate their lunch before putting on the second coat of paint.

Melissa shook her head. She'd been back at home for half an hour before the painting crew had returned. She and Anita had talked for a long time about the miscarriage and their relationship, and gone a long way toward understanding some of the rifts that had developed between them.

"No, you didn't." She looked at him over her slice of pizza. "You mean…?"

"They told her she couldn't stay unless she got rid of her Chihuahua."

"Why?"

Blue said, "No pets allowed in the single-room-occupancy hotels."

"Where's she going to live?"

Kyle shrugged. "The streets. Or the woods somewhere. I think she's got a campsite lined up."

"She chose the streets over housing?"

"She chose the dog over housing."

"They're going to freeze. Both of them."

"Especially that little dog. I tried to talk her out of it.…"

"Poor woman."

When the painting began again, Melissa took herself off to the hospital for her overnight shift.

MELISSA WENT TO SEE her father on her way home from work. He met her at the door and led her into the kitchen, where seed and plant catalogs were spread over the kitchen table.

Melissa made them both cups of herbal tea from a stash of dried mint he'd grown that summer. When he wasn't at work, Ben Lopez loved to spend time in his garden. Melissa had inherited from him not only a love of being outdoors but also an understanding of the cycle of the seasons.

And of her place in it.

The concept was simple—if you wanted a harvest, you had to plant your seeds at the right moment. Most of the time that was obvious—in the winter, with snow on the ground, your thoughts turned toward summer and it was easy to visualize what kind of a garden you would want to have, what crops to plant.

Some crops took more planning. Garlic, for instance. To plant garlic you had to be thinking of the following summer almost before the first one was done. The growing season was ten months long.

While her father told her about his plans for his garden, Melissa followed along in the seed catalog, imagining the procession of flowers in the backyard, changing week by week.

She would bring her child here in the summers. Her father's backyard would be a special place for her son or daughter to play. And her father, she knew, would make a terrific grandfather.

As they went out to her father's greenhouse, an addition to the back of the house he'd built himself, Melissa said, "My baby will be here this summer to see all your flowers."

Her father smiled at that prospect. "I'll grow extra black-eyed Susans, then. You always loved those when you were little."

The greenhouse was warm. Heat from the radiator system mixed with the warmth from whatever winter sunlight Portland was lucky enough to get.

Overhead lamps, color balanced to match the sun, supplied light when the sun didn't cooperate.

Her father had basil growing, green and strong. And other herbs: thyme, rosemary, cilantro. His planter baskets of flowers overwintered in here.

He was doing okay. Everything functional. She didn't want to disturb that. He wasn't the best at talking about feelings.

But she didn't know how to dance around what she wanted to say. She wanted to reassure him, to make him feel better, and she didn't know how to do it.

She had never known how to do it. But she had always felt it was her responsibility. Ever since she'd been eight years old.

Not knowing what to say brought back the same powerless feeling she'd had when she'd known he was contemplating suicide. She hadn't known what to say or do that could stop him then, and the waiting, during those months, had been brutal. Waiting and hoping and preparing herself for the possibility of another loss.

It had been too much, she thought, for an eight-year-old girl to take on. Particularly an eight-year-old who had just lived through the experiences she had.

Her father handed her a basil leaf. She crushed it between in her fingers and inhaled the licoricey summertime smell. She looked out into the garden.

Her father spoke. "I shouldn't have been so hard on her."

His words took her by surprise. She didn't say anything, just watched him as he went to the sink and filled his small metal watering can, the one with the long spout. Two ferns on the highest shelf got the first bit of water.

He was precise in his movements. Giving his plants what they needed to survive. No—more than that. Giving them what they needed to thrive. Sunlight and water and nutrients. And attention.

Melissa stared. "Dad. You don't think you caused Anita's miscarriage, do you?"

"I disapproved."

He said it as if it was the last word. As if there was nothing else to say. *I disapproved and she knew it and she has never been strong.*

"It wasn't your fault," she said.

"I disapproved of her living with Troy. Of her refusal to marry him. Of her being pregnant without a husband."

Melissa felt the sudden urge to shake him. This man who had been in her life for so long, whose beliefs were not hers but whose ability to rip himself apart surpassed even her own. "Just as you disapproved of my being pregnant before getting married."

"That was different."

"How?"

He didn't have to say it. *Because you could han-*

dle it. You're the strong one. The one who always holds it together, no matter what.

Right, she thought. *Because I'm the strong one.*

"It doesn't work that way, Dad. Some fetuses aren't viable. The body knows it and miscarries. So things can start again. A second chance."

A second chance was what none of them had gotten. Not after the truck.

"Okay," he said, and she knew she hadn't reached him. Nothing had changed.

"Dad, if parental displeasure could cause miscarriages, there wouldn't be six billion people on this planet."

He refilled his watering can. Melissa got the sense that more was going on here than she realized. But she didn't know what it was.

She remembered a statistic from her baby books. "Almost forty percent of women have a miscarriage at some point. It's hard and sad, but it's natural. Anita will get pregnant again. Married or not. With Troy or with someone else. You can be there for her then. Be there for her now."

The way you could be for me, if you wanted. She let the words go unspoken, tried not to project them. It wasn't her father's fault that he didn't seem all that interested in her baby. He had cried at her wedding, but after that everything was business as usual. His treatment of Kyle had not changed significantly; it had always been good.

Because she had proved herself to be the strong

one. The one who gave help, not the one who ever needed support, or visible demonstrations of love. She had made it that way. Any other instincts had been trained out of him, trained out of Anita.

But not out of Kyle.

He had seen her as weak as she ever got, and he had comforted her and he had married her.

And that had to stand for something.

THAT NIGHT KYLE came over and the three of them had dinner at her father's. She and her father didn't mention their conversation from earlier. It was as if it hadn't happened.

After dinner she and Kyle went over to Kyle's old apartment.

His apartment looked like a ghost town. The living room contained just the couch and the ficus. His bedroom just the bed. The muslin curtains still hung from the windows, but the only illumination came from the overhead fixtures. The place looked stark and empty, nothing like the apartment she had spent every Wednesday evening in for the past few years.

Her mind was still lingering on the conversations she'd had with her sister and father.

She said to Kyle, "If we ever lose our child, for any reason, I'm going to need your support."

His brow furrowed, as if he didn't know quite where the question was coming from or why it was coming right at this moment. "You'll have it."

"Your absolute and total support. Regardless of who's to blame. Regardless of how you feel. You'll have to be my friend."

Kyle went to his couch and sat down. He motioned to the cushion next to him, urging her down. She sat next to him, almost touching.

"We've always depended on each other," he said. "It won't be any different."

That was true. They had depended on each other in the past. But the way they'd done it had hardly been the best way possible.

Look at what had happened in July. They'd each had traumatic experiences that day, but instead of talking about them they'd jumped into bed. Physical needs had taken over. Had sent them running from the facts of what had happened, burying them.

I lost a five-year-old boy tonight, was all she'd been able to say. The boy had been so much like her own brother. Telling his mother had been incredibly painful.

Kyle had held her and kissed her and then everything had gone up in flames like an abandoned house torched by an arsonist. Minutes later they'd been in bed together. Any chance of talking about their feelings like reasonable adults was gone.

No talking, just a crazy fire that had sprung up as if out of nowhere. Once he'd kissed her all she'd had to do was kiss him back and they'd been lost. Both of them elsewhere, soothing their own broken selves with each other's bodies. Losing themselves in the heat. Craving release from the things that imprisoned them.

Kyle hadn't said anything about his feelings that night, but she'd known it was the anniversary of Felicity's death. She'd felt his desperation in his body, had tried to console him.

They'd given each other comfort.

That she was already in love with him, even then, had helped, of course, though the knowledge had still been unconscious. Otherwise she never would have let the physical intimacy happen. She'd figured *that* out.

But making love hadn't really fixed anything. It had just pushed the painful emotions away under the sensual haze of desire.

"Where is this coming from?" Kyle asked.

"From always having to be the strong one," she admitted. "And from the problems Anita and Troy have been having. And from the way she keeps blaming herself for the miscarriage."

She told him about her sister's feelings of guilt. And her father's. Feelings that had resisted her attempts to soothe them away.

"That's natural, isn't it?" he asked. "To want to affix blame for bad things that happen? Even if it means blaming ourselves?"

"Even if it's so obviously untrue?"

Kyle put his hand on her knee. "You've never blamed yourself for something?"

"I've never blamed myself for something that wasn't my fault," she answered. Honest. Trying to hide the rawness. Not realizing what she'd revealed until he spoke again.

She could hear a smile in his voice. "Maybe you'd better tell me what you blame yourself for."

"No, thanks."

"That bad, huh?"

She didn't answer.

Kyle examined her face. Her face, which probably gave away her feelings. "Melissa."

She turned her head.

"Melissa, look at me."

She did.

"What's going on?"

"Nothing," she said. "Forget I even opened my mouth."

"What do you blame yourself for?"

"Just drop it, Kyle."

"Melissa, nothing you could tell me could make me think less of you. We're friends. I support you completely."

She felt herself growing agitated. "Then support me by not talking about it."

Kyle put his arm on the back of the couch. He leaned toward her.

She didn't back away. She knew she was losing this battle. That she'd lost it the moment she'd revealed her sense of guilt. Kyle might be easygoing in many respects, but he could also be tenacious.

"I think I'd rather support you by having you get it off your chest," he said.

She watched him. Trying to see into him. This was her husband and they had a strange shell of a marriage, but if she couldn't trust him, then who could she trust?

And maybe turning to him would make their marriage more real. It wouldn't make him love her, but at least he would know the real person inside her.

She thought of his words the day she had told him she was pregnant.

Who takes care of you? Who do you turn to?

Him, of course.

But she'd never given him the chance.

So give him the chance, she told herself. If he couldn't handle it, better to find out now.

"Fine, then."

She opened her mouth to tell him. The words stuck in her throat. Her mouth worked, but nothing happened; no sound came out.

"It's okay," he said, his voice like a cool cloth on fevered skin.

She faltered, her courage wavering. "You don't really want to know this."

"I do."

Something in his voice convinced her. The quiet

steadiness. Or maybe it was the way he was looking at her, his expression caring and receptive.

She tried again. The words came out a little quivery. She had never said these words to any living person. "The accident. It was—"

"Yes?"

"It was my fault."

And then she felt as if she were in free fall, as if the couch and the floor and the ground and everything else dependable in her world had just disappeared and nothing was holding her up anymore.

She tumbled, end over end, into an abyss.

CHAPTER FIFTEEN

HER THOUGHTS WERE barely coherent. She felt as if Kyle would leave her now. That the horror of being married to someone who had basically killed her own mother and her little brother would be too much for him. He wouldn't want their child to be raised by someone like her.

He would divorce her and take their child away, said that primitive, irrational part of herself. *Your Honor, she's not a fit parent. She killed her own mother.*

But Kyle did not run screaming from the room. He sat on the couch, steady as a rock and said, "The accident when you were eight years old?"

"Yes."

"Tell me why you think that."

"Because it's true."

"Mel..."

She thought back to the accident. An ordinary day driving down an ordinary road, and in the space of ten seconds everything in her life had changed. Everything.

"Tell me about it," he said.

"I distracted her," she said. "I was being a brat.

Bothering Charlie. He was sitting in the passenger seat and I was behind him. I was fiddling with his hair and dropping scraps of paper on him.''

"And?"

"Mom tried to get me to stop, but I wouldn't. I was getting trash all over the car and making Charlie start to cry and I just didn't stop."

"It sounds like you were being eight years old," Kyle said. "Go on."

"And she finally got so fed up she turned around to give me the eye. You know, to make me see that she meant it when she told me to be quiet."

"That's when the truck came?"

"Yeah. That's when the truck came."

Kyle reached out and pulled her onto his lap. For some reason the action felt incredibly natural. Probably because her thoughts were elsewhere, in the back of that car.

He held her against him. "It's okay," he murmured. "It's okay."

She accepted his comfort for a moment. But only a moment. "No, it's definitely not okay. If I hadn't been being a brat, the accident wouldn't have happened."

Kyle was silent for a while, holding her. Then he asked, "What part of the truck did you hit?"

"The back corner." She'd stared at it in shock for most of the forty-five minutes it took the fire department to cut them out.

"Did your mother swerve into another lane when she turned to talk to you?"

"No, but…"

"You must have hit the truck pretty hard."

"Yeah. There wasn't really any time to brake. It just came out of nowhere."

"So you were moving fast?"

"Yeah."

He said, "I bet you didn't know a lot about stopping distances when you were eight years old. But you know about them now. If you hit that hard, I don't think even a few seconds more lead time would have made any difference."

"It might have."

"Even so, you were just being an eight-year-old girl. Just an ordinary girl doing ordinary things that kids do. Craig and I were monsters to each other sometimes. It doesn't make you responsible for the accident any more than Anita was responsible for her miscarriage. It wasn't your fault."

She wasn't ready to hear him yet. She couldn't hear him. His words made sense, but she kept hearing the squeal of the tires on the pavement as her mother tried in vain to stop.

Kyle was still holding her. She tried to slip out of his lap but he held her fast. "Relax, Melissa. Don't run away."

"Don't you see? I *want* to run away."

"It hurts to lose people."

Something inside her fractured. "You're

damned right it hurts to lose people.'' The pitch of her voice rose. She felt it going out of her control. ''And it hurts even more when you're trapped in the car with them and they're dying and you're eight years old and you can't do a damned thing to save them!''

And you know it's your fault.

Kyle held her close. ''Oh, Mel.''

''It hurts,'' she said. Her voice sounded broken. She felt broken.

''I know it does.''

And then somehow they were kissing.

She didn't know who started it and she didn't care. Probably her. He was just so close, and she knew it wouldn't make things any better, but she couldn't resist.

The heat between them was instant. The kiss was nothing like the anemic kiss in the church, or that softly seductive kiss they'd shared before that.

This kiss was just like July.

Hot. Irresistible.

It left no chance of stopping.

Her emotions were just like the ones she'd felt in July. Overwhelming despair. Regret. Loss.

Make it go away, Kyle. Help me make it go away.

And he did.

He took her to the bedroom and made slow love to her. Late into the night. Until she was too tired to think anymore, too tired to feel.

SHE WOKE UP IN HIS ARMS.

That in itself wasn't so unusual. It was the getting there....

Being in his apartment. Obviously there was something about the place that worked a little magic on her self-control.

At least I didn't tell him I loved him. She had to be thankful for small mercies.

She hadn't gotten all that much sleep, but she felt well rested. Maybe the no-sex thing had been overrated, she told herself.

Kyle stirred. He opened his eyes. Looked at her. "Not a dream, then," he said, sleepy and husky.

"You've been dreaming of making love to me?"

"Every damned night."

And he didn't sound particularly pleased with himself for it.

She laughed. "Poor boy."

"Yeah. Well, I don't think you planned on having a husband who takes advantage of you when you're in emotionally overwrought states."

"I didn't mind. Anyway, who's to say I didn't take advantage of you?"

"You're not regretting last night." An observation, not a question.

No, she wasn't regretting last night. How could she regret making love to him, as long as she hadn't said anything stupid?

But she decided to keep playing it nonchalant, to pretend it didn't mean much.

"We're married," she said. "We're friends. We knew it was going to happen eventually."

"Okay," he said.

"God, listen to me. I sound like such a *guy*."

"I beg to differ."

"No, I mean it. Guys are all into friendly sex. You know. You like someone. You're attracted. Why not do it? No big deal. No love required. It's like going for a bike ride or playing Frisbee. Same level of commitment."

He raised an eyebrow. "Interesting theory."

"Well, you have to remember I observed you in action for five years."

"Ouch."

"Why ouch? It's a good skill for when you marry your best friend."

She got up out of bed, naked, fighting a burst of self-consciousness that would have put the lie to what she'd just said. Her clothes were on the floor where they'd discarded them last night.

She put them on, thinking back to her confession the night before. She didn't feel any less at fault, but it had been nice of Kyle to listen to her without judgment.

"I'm pretty hungry," she said. "What do you say we get out of this bachelor pad and go back home, where we can get something to eat?"

"Sure," he said. "But, Melissa…"

"Hmm?"

"One thing." He sat up in the bed, the sheets down around his waist. "Two nights like last night definitely makes us lovers. We won't be going back to that platonic arrangement we had."

ANITA CAME OVER the next day. She brought a pad of sketching paper on her oversized clipboard.

"I'm going to draw you now," she said. And there was something in her voice that made Melissa hear an unspoken addition to the sentence. *I'm going to draw the real you.*

Not quite the real me, she thought. But close.

Kyle had gone to the clinic for a while. Melissa sat in a chair in the living room, with a window to the backyard beside her.

Anita sketched as they talked, her strokes bold.

"How's Troy?" Melissa asked.

"And maybe you want an honest answer today?"

"Yeah. That would be good."

"Ooh. Nice smile. Hold that for a second."

Melissa tried to, but she was afraid it turned into more of a grimace in the thirty seconds Anita drew it.

Anita took out a fresh sheet of paper.

"Troy's fine," she said. A pause while she put down a few strokes. Then, meeting Melissa's eyes, she added, "It's things between us that aren't so good."

"Since the miscarriage?"

"Yeah."

They were silent for a moment, sharing the sadness.

"He wants to marry me." She said it as if it were something bad.

"That's a problem?"

Anita didn't answer for a long time. She stared at Melissa with her artist's expression, then went back to the sketch.

After a few minutes she put her charcoal down and turned the sketch pad around so Melissa could see it.

The drawing was incredible. It caught something ineffable, focused in on some pure joy of future motherhood. And yet there was a sadness behind it. An awareness of love lost. Melissa felt that Anita had captured their entire conversation from a few days earlier in the strokes of her charcoal.

Her eyes stung. "How do you *do* that?"

"I'm no one he should marry."

It took a second for Melissa to remember her question. *That's a problem?* That he wants to marry you?

"Why?"

"Because. Of who I am."

"Who are you?"

"Panic attacks. Freak-outs." She met Melissa's gaze. "Total emotional blindness."

"Bullshit."

"You're my sister. You have to say that."

"Does he know you?"

"Yes." Reluctant.

"Do you keep secrets from him? Have you concealed your panic, your freak-outs?"

"No."

"Then maybe you *are* the person he should marry."

Anita removed the sketch from her pad. She put it on the floor beside the chair.

"I want that," Melissa said, pointing.

"Okay."

"I mean it. I really want it."

Anita picked up her charcoal. "We can go frame it together. If you really like it."

"I like it."

"Good. I'm glad."

They shared a sisterly smile.

Suddenly Melissa knew she couldn't keep quiet anymore about her secret. She'd kept it far too long, and it was time to risk putting it out in the open. To return the confidence that Anita had had in her when she'd opened up the other day.

"Anita," she began. "I've got something I need to tell you. It's about the car accident with Mom and Charlie."

TWO PEOPLE KNEW her secret now, Melissa thought. Neither had believed she was responsible, but that didn't really surprise her. No one wanted to blame an eight-year-old girl for two deaths.

She felt lighter, though. As if telling other people had made the burden somehow easier to bear. She hadn't realized how hard keeping the secret had been. How lonely it had made her feel.

ALL WEEK KYLE THOUGHT about Melissa's confession.

He'd known the loss of her mother and brother had scarred her, but he'd never imagined she would have put herself through such hell about it for so many years.

The things we do for love, and out of pain...

No wonder she'd taken on the role of being strong in the family. She hadn't let herself share the sense of loss her sister and father had felt. Her grief had been private, unacknowledged. And she'd created a situation where no one comforted her for her loss, because she didn't think she deserved it.

How misguided was that?

And how totally, typically Melissa...

Part of her probably didn't even think she deserved love. And that, he realized, might have something to do with why she had never sought out relationships. And why she had agreed to marry her best friend.

It was a lot to think about during his busy week at work. On Thursday afternoon he had an appointment at the other end of downtown with one of his board members to review the clinic's budget.

Blue dropped by the clinic just before he left, so Kyle invited him along for the walk.

A few days earlier Blue had put himself on the waiting list for a long-term transitional shelter. He'd be able to stay six months if he kept his act together.

A lot of kids on the street weren't able to do it. The lure of drugs and other things was too hard to resist. So many free hours without direction were hard to fill in positive ways. Easy to fill in negative ones.

Kyle had found himself really liking the once-sullen kid. Their experience preparing and painting the baby's room had cemented something between them. Kyle felt like an unofficial big brother to the boy, who was smart, a good worker and a good talker. And he wasn't half-bad at basketball, which he had played earlier in the week with Kyle and Jerome.

"Someday, Blue," Kyle said to him as they walked along through the riverfront park by the Willamette River, "you're going to want to tell me your real name."

Their route was the most scenic way to get to the high-rise where the board member, an architect, worked. Especially on a moderately sunny day.

"Matt Henry," Blue said, just like that. Kyle supposed he had earned the kid's trust.

''Why 'Blue'?''

Blue shrugged. ''I was wearing a blue raincoat when I got off the bus.''

''You want to be called Matt?''

''Blue is good.''

Blue, Kyle thought, was the boy in Portland, the boy who had traveled out here on the bus and somehow landed mostly on his feet. Matt was someone he'd left behind.

He thought about what else Blue had left behind. ''Do your parents know where you are?''

''Nah.''

''Think they're worried?''

Blue shrugged. ''Maybe for a while. But it's not like they'd put my face on a milk carton. Even if my mom thought of it, my stepdad wouldn't let her.''

''I would if you were my kid,'' Kyle said.

Blue didn't say anything. Kyle glanced over. He was staring straight ahead, as if he hadn't heard Kyle.

Interesting.

''You want me to call them, don't you?'' Blue asked at last.

''Your mom might be worried.''

''Yeah, well, my stepfather certainly doesn't give a shit.''

''Okay. You want to call your mother?''

Blue scuffed his shoe on the cement. ''She's not a very independent person.''

"Meaning?" It either meant she was disabled in some way, or...

"My stepfather's got her under his thumb."

Kyle was silent. They passed a fountain, dry for the winter, where children played in the summertime. Where his child would play someday, with other children from all over the city, enjoying water on a hot summer day. "Does he hit her?" he asked.

"Nah. Only me." He looked away. "He just talks down to her, gives her a hard time. Won't let her do what she wants. She loves him anyway. I don't get that."

Kyle didn't get it, either. "Love is strange," he said.

Profound, Kyle. Real profound.

"People stay together for all kinds of reasons," he added. "Not all of them make sense."

"Especially to a teenager, you mean?"

"To anyone. Sometimes to the people themselves." He pretended that he wasn't speaking from experience, that he wasn't confused about his own relationship, that his reasons for making a marriage with Melissa made any kind of sense to an outside observer. Blue obviously thought they had a strong marriage, a real marriage.

Blue said, "Yeah. Whatever it is, people are pretty screwed up sometimes."

Kyle laughed. "No kidding."

They were almost at the architect's building.

"I'll probably be here a couple of hours," he told Blue. "You got any plans for the afternoon?"

Blue shrugged. "Just kicking around."

Kyle had a better idea. "The library isn't too far away. Ten blocks, maybe. I'll swing by and check the periodical room after my meeting. If you're there, we can go grab some pizza."

Blue nodded, then began to walk that way. He turned back ten feet away and said, "You can call her if you want. I don't care."

CHAPTER SIXTEEN

December

OVER THE NEXT MONTH Kyle started to feel that he and Melissa were really *married*. At times it freaked him out more than others. But it wasn't such a bad thing to be married to your friend. They got along well. Rarely argued. Enjoyed the same television shows.

And the sex was good, too. Not as incendiary as in July and on their first night together after that, but still good.

He'd moved his dresser into her bedroom. The photo of Felicity he'd stashed in a desk drawer.

It was getting colder as winter settled in. He sometimes saw Zita at Buddy's. She was living in an abandoned warehouse and her blood pressure was high. She would leave Frank in a blanket on the sidewalk out front, dart in to order her food in reused take-out containers and then eat it on the sidewalk so she could be with Frank.

Kyle knew that the people who worked at Buddy's would love to help Zita by letting her dog come in, but health-code regulations were strict.

They risked having the entire restaurant get shut down if they allowed a violation like that.

One of the other customers at the café had once raised dogs. He spent time with Zita and Frank on the sidewalk and estimated Frank's age at about six. Not a spring chicken for a Chihuahua.

When he took time to think about it, Kyle marveled at the affection between the dog and human. Not just the affection he saw in front of him from the otherwise difficult woman, but the sheer fact that she would choose a dog over housing. A dog she'd known only a few months. A dog that would die in a few years, probably, especially under the stresses of living on the street.

That was love, and sacrifice. And risk.

MELISSA WAS GROWING BIG by Christmas. Just as her father had predicted.

They had a quiet Christmas Eve dinner at her father's house. It snowed. Anita and Troy were in California with his parents and siblings.

Anita was considering marrying him.

Melissa was glad for her. Her relationship with Anita was better than it had been for a long time.

She stepped outside while Kyle and her father talked in the living room. The backyard was quiet in the drifting snowfall. The snow hadn't been falling long, and was only an inch or so at its deepest. Closer to the house, by the sliding-glass door, it melted as soon as it fell, leaving a wet sheen.

The security light on the side of the house cast a wide beam of yellow light down through the snow, illuminating the sculpted folds of her father's backyard.

Winter.

Melissa had changed her routine at the hospital so she worked exclusively days now, with some early-morning and late-evening shifts. Nothing overnight. It meant that she'd had to cut back on her Wednesday hours at the clinic, but she probably would have had to do that anyway. She couldn't grow a baby and keep the same schedule.

The sliding door opened and closed. Kyle stepped toward her on the porch. She could hear his footfalls on the boards, the sound muted by the snow. She could feel the planks flex under his weight.

Kyle. Solid Kyle.

Whose feelings for her hadn't changed. Still friends and nothing more. Just as she'd expected.

He stood beside her at the railing. Put a hand on her shoulder. "Warm enough?"

She nodded. They weren't reaching each other. Would never reach each other.

She felt a sense of dread building inside her. Someday this whole house of cards they called a marriage would come tumbling down around them. She loved Kyle, but he didn't love her back. He never would.

And though their relationship seemed to be going forward just as they'd planned, Melissa had her doubts. Kyle had never been good at long-term relationships, not while she'd known him and not before, if his stories were anything to go by.

She could almost endure it if their marriage never changed. If it was always this strange balance of friendship, desire and hidden love.

But it wouldn't stay the same. It couldn't possibly stay the same.

And she felt herself starting to pull away from him. To protect herself from the loss she feared.

THEY DROVE HOME in silence through the lightening snow. By the time they reached the house only isolated flakes dropped out of the sky, drifting down through the white glow of the streetlights.

The city looked magical in a snowfall like this, she thought. All too often Oregon was gray and wet in the winter. Snow, especially at the holiday, was a precious commodity. It changed things, made them look fresh and different. Erased the familiar landmarks and created a new landscape.

She got out of the car. Kyle joined her. He reached down and scooped up a handful of snow. It was just cold enough for it to be slightly dry, not mushy and wet. He touched the snow to his tongue.

"Snow ice cream," she said.

He dropped the handful of snow. "Next winter."

Snow ice cream, at least the way they had made it in the past, involved raw eggs. Not something she could subject her pregnant body to. No matter how delicious the rare treat was.

Kyle followed her up the walk to the house. He had his keys out and unlocked the door for her. They turned on lights, kicked the thermostat back up. It wasn't very late. Nine-thirty. In years past she'd gone to midnight services with Anita and her father. One of her rare appearances in church.

Not tonight. That was too late to be out, with the way she got tired late at night.

She shed her coat, feeling five miles away from him, even though he was close enough to touch. Dinner had been inconsequential, the conversation typical family talk. No substance that she could remember; they had all been a bit subdued.

Saying nothing, she headed for the kitchen. Put the kettle on for tea, then changed her mind. Changed it back again.

He ambled in a moment later. The kettle was on the stove, with the gas turned up high underneath it. It made a sound, the sort of settling, glowing sound as the first round of tiny bubbles released themselves from the bottom. The sound quieted slightly, ready to build slowly to the noisy boil, where it would once again soften.

She took a box of tea from the cupboard by the stove. Removed a tea bag and put it in a mug, her motions careful. Chamomile tea. Soothing and calming for nighttime.

And how she needed that.

He was watching her.

"What?"

"Nothing." Shaking his head. "Just you."

She couldn't read him. Vulnerability swept over her.

She took the water off early. Lukewarm. The tea was weakly yellow. "I need a shower."

She carried the cup with her. In the bathroom she turned on the hot-water tap, then waited with her finger in the stream for the water to heat up, before turning on the spray. She stepped out of her clothes, sipped tepid tea, then put the cup by the sink.

She thought of what Anita had said to her after her confession. That she didn't need to always be the strong one anymore.

It was a nice thought, but she didn't really know how not to be.

And she couldn't get through twenty years of this marriage without being strong.

Because Kyle could walk away.

She shouldn't keep doing this to herself, shouldn't keep asking for this pattern to repeat, this pain to threaten.

The water sluiced through her hair, warming her. She soaped up, rubbing her round belly. Sometimes she almost thought she could handle being a mother. Loving a being who would all too soon be independent of her. Crossing streets. Going to school. Making friends. Doing all sorts of dangerous things. And she would have to work and wait and prepare herself to keep on living even if her child didn't.

No matter what happened, she knew she would never choose to end her own life. She thought of her father, who had flirted with the idea but had finally resisted it, and had made a decent life for himself without his wife. Maybe he was stronger than she'd thought he was. Strong enough to stay alive. For Anita. And for her.

Melissa rinsed off and shut the taps. She stood for a minute, dripping. Then she dried herself and got into bed.

Kyle joined her in a few minutes. She was on her side, watching him. He was on his side, too, propped up on one elbow. Looking down at her. Smiling.

"Merry Christmas," he said.

She swallowed. They made love more often now, without the heat of emotional trauma to drive them to it. It was good, comfortable.

"Come here."

She scooted closer. He reached out and settled a large warm hand on her rib cage. The contact drew all her awareness, felt incredibly sensual.

He leaned closer and kissed her on the lips. A floating kiss at first, meeting her and getting reacquainted. Then it became stronger, that hand of his still on her rib cage, anchoring her. She kissed him back, forgetting herself, letting it happen.

The pleasure grew and intensified. Reminding her of July, and of all the nights since then.

She was just like anyone else. She wanted someone to hold her and caress her and take her away from herself. Someone to share this with.

Desire flared, but with it came panic. She felt it steal in, gain a foothold, like a virus multiplying in a host cell. The population doubling with every generation.

She tried to fight it back but couldn't. It was too much of an old friend, too constant a presence in her life. The fear of living with the truth. The fear of someday forgiving herself. Moving on. Being different than she'd always been.

Because no matter whether it was her fault or not, she had still lost her mother and brother that day.

And she would lose Kyle.

Kyle was touching her. Her body, at least, responded. Arousal, engorgement. All the clinical signs of pleasure were there, but all she could see was the panic, a watercolor wash of red.

They made love. He was a strong and tender lover. He drew out her response, tormented her with the edge of release and then brought her to orgasm with himself inside her and her body pulsing around him.

And it wasn't enough.

CHAPTER SEVENTEEN

KYLE LAY IN BED, awake, after Melissa had dropped off.

Something felt wrong. How could you be so close to someone and be so damned far away? It wasn't that sex between them was mechanical. Far from it. She wasn't just going through the motions. No, she was there with him, all right, but there was some kind of wall between them. A place she didn't let him touch.

This was what he wanted, wasn't it? Friendship and sex.

But something was missing.

He kept asking himself, tonight and other nights, *Is this all there is?*

He was thirty-two years old and he'd never had that thought before Melissa.

She was the mother of his child. His wife. Things should be different, but he didn't know how they ought to be, or how to make them so.

As KYLE UNWRAPPED the presents she'd bought him, Melissa thought about her reactions the night before. Her despair, which she'd kept hidden.

Her own words to Anita, weeks ago, went around in her head.

Do you keep secrets from him?

Anita had said no. She didn't keep secrets from Troy. And they would probably end up happily married, with a relationship that was much stronger and truer than the one Melissa shared with Kyle.

Unlike Anita, she couldn't answer that question in the negative. She did keep secrets from Kyle. Maybe she'd told him about the accident, about what she'd done to cause it. But she loved him. And she still hadn't told him so.

But how did you tell a man that? Especially when the man was your husband.

And especially when he couldn't return your feelings.

It wasn't even that she didn't understand *why* he couldn't love her. Why friendship was all he would be able to offer.

He had been abandoned two times too many.

While she…

Well, her father had stuck it out, hadn't he? She'd been terrified he would leave her. That she would come home from school one day and find him dead, or wake up with him gone. If she was a good enough student, she'd thought, if she did everything right, then maybe he wouldn't leave her.

And he *hadn't* left her.

But Kyle's father had. And so had his fiancée.

So even though her feelings for Kyle weren't going to change—they could hardly get stronger, and falling out of love with him didn't seem like a possibility, either—she continued to keep her secret.

ON THE DAY AFTER CHRISTMAS, the phone rang in the afternoon. Kyle picked up on the first ring.

"Kyle Davenport?" a male voice asked.

"Yes." He could hear noise in the background, chaos.

"This is Mercy Hospital calling…"

Kyle's stomach clenched. Mercy was a hospital near downtown, not far from where Melissa and Anita had gone shopping to pick up postholiday bargains.

"There's a woman here who asked us to call you." Kyle heard the sound of flipping pages, as if the man were looking for the name. "Susan Smith. She keeps muttering something about some dog."

Kyle took a deep breath. "Zita," he said, half to himself.

"Actually, I think the dog's name is Frank. That's the name she keeps saying."

"I meant the woman. What's wrong with her?"

He could hear the man's shrug clear through the telephone line. "Looks like pretty severe hypothermia. Maybe other stuff, as well. She's not doing so hot."

Damn. "Where's the dog?"

"Not a clue."

"It didn't come in on the ambulance?"

"No way. Police found her. You might want to ask them."

Kyle called the downtown station and waited to speak to someone who could help him. His relief that it wasn't Melissa in trouble was strong, but he was also worried about Zita and Frank. If they'd gotten caught out in the pre-Christmas snowstorm, things could be pretty hard for them.

Finally he got hold of someone who could help him. "The dog was taken to the pound," a woman told him. "You want their number?"

Half an hour later he had reached the pound and gotten the assurance of the desk clerk that Frank was alive and would remain that way for the next few hours at least.

He waited for Melissa to come home. "Interested in another trip out?" he asked her when she and Anita arrived.

She gave him an are-you-crazy look, but asked anyway, "What for?"

Kyle explained the situation.

"Of course I'll come. And we'll go see Zita afterward."

Anita went, too.

Anita, who had become like some kind of watchdog in the past few weeks. He almost expected her to growl whenever he came near.

ZITA WAS HER CRANKY SELF. They snuck the dog—which was in less than optimal health—into her room. Zita herself was barely functional, and could only see them for a moment or two.

"Leave Frank here with me," she told them. "I'll take care of her.

She looked a full thirty years older than she had a few weeks earlier.

"We'll look after Frank," Kyle assured her.

ZITA'S HEART STOPPED late that night.

The hospital phoned with the news in the morning. "There's no next of kin," the nurse told him.

Kyle looked down into his lap, where the three-legged Chihuahua licked her nose with a long pink tongue.

Oh, yes there is.

MELISSA TOOK the little dog over to her father's house a few days later, on the off chance that he would fall madly in love with the animal and demand to adopt it.

No such luck.

"That's sort of cute," he said, looking down at Frank. "Why don't we shut it in the kitchen and take a walk."

"It's a she," Melissa said.

"Hmm."

She and Kyle planned to keep the dog for only a couple of days. Kyle had put in some calls, trying to find someone who wanted a three-legged Chihuahua, skin and bones but very sweet.

Nobody wanted her.

The animal shelter said they could put her up for adoption, but if no one wanted her she'd be destroyed. Melissa and Kyle had taken her over. They'd left her in the car while they went to inspect the cages.

Everything was clean, but when they went back out to the car, they'd gotten in and driven away. They couldn't do that to Frank, not after the way Zita had loved her, and not after the sacrifices she'd made to be with her.

"We'll just have to keep trying to find her a home," Melissa had said.

Neither of them had ever owned pets, not as adults, so they didn't really consider keeping her as a permanent part of their family.

January

AFTER THE NEW YEAR, Kyle finally called Blue's mother in Missoula. He picked a time when he thought the stepfather would be out and pressed a code into his phone to conceal his phone number.

A woman answered.

"Mrs. Stevens?" Kyle asked. Her last name was different from Blue's.

"Yeah? Who's this?"

"My name is Kyle Davenport. You don't know me."

"Okay."

"I just wanted to tell you that your son is okay. He's living in Portland and he works for me some afternoons."

"Oh," she said.

Kyle waited, a long time, for her to say something else.

She didn't.

"He's doing okay," Kyle said again. "He's a good kid."

"Yeah," the woman said.

Kyle hung up the phone, wondering if that was how his father would have reacted to news of Craig and him. The absence of any feeling was hard to fathom.

But some people were just that way.

Not him.

He wouldn't abandon a son or daughter. Even if he and Melissa for some reason couldn't live with each other, he would still stick around in his child's life.

Unlike his father.

He felt a sudden wave of anger for the man who had disappeared from his life. As a child he had been so...confused by his father's absence. He'd never focused on the anger and the feelings of betrayal.

What his father had done was unacceptable. His

were the actions of a man who had no conception of love, no capacity for it.

He had turned his back on his family. Something Kyle would never do.

February

FRANK WAS STILL WITH THEM. "I think we have a dog," Melissa said.

"What dog?" Kyle asked. "All I see is an overgrown rat." Frank turned circles on the rug, then trotted over to the hardwood floor and threw up.

Frank, it turned out, had a voracious appetite and a sensitive stomach.

Kyle sighed. "My turn to clean it up."

Melissa smiled and cupped her rounded belly. "Good practice for later."

March

"I DON'T EVEN WANT to *know* what's in here," Melissa said as she held the small gift-wrapped package from the head of the nursing staff.

The staff at the hospital had arranged a baby shower for her.

"Open it," one of the nurses urged.

She glanced at Sarah Upton, the head nurse. The woman grinned mischievously.

Melissa had attended other baby showers at the

hospital. She knew roughly what to expect. "It's not for the baby, is it?"

"Uh-uh."

She put the package back down, blushing. "Sarah, there's no way I can open this here."

General laughter. "Open it later, then. At home with Kyle."

Melissa smiled and put the package on the unwrapped stack of baby supplies she'd received from her friends at the hospital. Unfortunately that wasn't an option. She'd be unwrapping whatever it was in the privacy of the bedroom when Kyle was not around, and no doubt hiding it deep in her underwear drawer.

The box probably contained a patent leather bustier or a pair of plastic handcuffs and a whip. Not the kind of thing she wanted to share with her husband.

Sarah, bless her heart, had a slightly off-kilter sense of humor.

Melissa patted her almost bursting stomach. "Whatever it is, I doubt I'll be able to fit into it for quite a while."

"A goal to shoot for," joked Amy, a fellow doctor in the hospital who'd given birth the year before.

Melissa had reached the impatient stage of pregnancy. It was all enough already. She felt as if she had a watermelon in her stomach. Everything had become uncomfortable, and the business of having to pee every fifteen minutes was beginning to get on her nerves.

And she wanted to see her baby.

At night, lying with Kyle in their big bed, she visualized again and again how the birth would go, how it would feel to hold her little infant in her arms. She felt powerful and maternal just thinking about it. And impatient, damn it!

April

SHE WAS WITH ANITA when her water broke. Anita, who should have been almost as big as her by now. They were at her apartment, relaxing, talking, when it happened. She had felt some slow contractions begin a few hours earlier, but they were too far apart for a trip to the hospital.

Until her water broke.

They called Kyle and went to the hospital. She'd handled the paperwork months ago and was immediately whisked to a delivery suite upstairs. Upstairs, in an area of the hospital where she never went, had no reason to go.

She gave birth to a daughter twelve hours afterward. They named her Emily after Kyle's maternal grandmother.

She had asked to have the baby given to her as soon as the medical checks were done. She wanted to provide the infant with a sense of security in her first moments.

The doctor handed Emily to her. Melissa looked into her little girl's eyes, took in the tiny nose and mouth, and she realized the enormity of what she'd done.

Something seemed to shatter inside her, as if her soul were a glass vessel under enormous pressure and someone had just tapped it with a hammer. It broke in on itself, the shards tumbling and spraying.

She'd thought she would be okay. In the past few months she'd done everything she could to keep herself calm. She'd reminded herself that women had been giving birth for centuries, and to lose your child before you died yourself was the exception, rather than the rule.

Even coming over to the hospital she'd felt as if she could handle this.

But she couldn't.

She held herself together, knowing that if she started to cry she wouldn't be able to stop. Kyle was there, and her sister, and Dr. Porter.

None of them noticed anything wrong. No one had ever noticed anything wrong.

The words spun around in her head. *I'm so afraid.*

They repeated, chained to her in a nightmare rhythm. *I'm so afraid. So afraid. So afraid.*

The baby, lying naked on the bare skin of her chest, a blanket over her, latched onto one of her nipples.

Kyle stroked their daughter's fuzzy head. She looked up at him. He met her gaze and smiled. Reassuring, happy.

Oh, Kyle, I'm so afraid.

AFTER AN HOUR the baby slept on Melissa's chest. Melissa dozed in the hospital bed, Kyle in the chair beside her. Everyone else had cleared out.

She slept fitfully, and her emotions were a tangle. She felt overpowering love for the girl sleeping so trustingly on her. But fear hovered like a shadow. Because it was dangerous to love people. So easy to lose them.

Melissa had been born in the same hospital, probably even on the same floor. Her mother had given birth three times. First to Anita, then herself, then Charlie.

Had her mother felt this mix of emotions afterward with each of them, or just elation? She had been a good mother. Tolerant and loving, able to set limits. Never mean, even when she was upset. All of which had made losing her even harder.

Kyle was watching her. Watching their baby girl. "What are you thinking about?" she asked.

Kyle's eyes softened. "How proud I am of you."

How proud. But not how much he loved her. She felt a moment of extraordinary weakness. Usually she was fine with their arrangement, but right now she wanted to be loved. Wanted to have someone help her through the terror she felt. Wanted someone to help her make it safe. Someone who could be there for her no matter what, and forgive her for anything.

She thought of how it had felt to make love these past few months. Each time since Christmas Melissa had fought the panic that welled up inside her.

It will always be like this, she'd realized. Never anything different, because their marriage would always be a half marriage. Something they'd done for the sake of Emily, and because they were friends.

But sometimes she worried their friendship would slip away. That they would become acquaintances sharing the same house, the same bed.

She closed her eyes, knowing she hadn't responded. Not caring. She had just given birth, and he would understand.

LATER THERE WERE other people at the hospital, and after she slept she saw them. Her father. Anita and Troy. Barbara. Jerome. Whitney.

Whitney wanted to hold the baby. "When we bring her home," Melissa said. She felt possessive for some reason, reluctant to let anyone but Kyle and essential medical personnel hold her.

Melissa endured her feelings. And was fearful. The horrifying fear came in waves. Mostly she was able to tamp it down, ignore it. Tell herself that she would get through it. That it was only this one child she had to worry about. And that Kyle must be going through similar emotions. Kyle, with his history.

Raising a child together would stretch them both. But they both wanted it like this. So they would both have to find a way to live with their circumstances.

Unfortunately that realization didn't bring comfort.

Because the fear never really went away.

CHAPTER EIGHTEEN

FRANK WAS OVERJOYED when Melissa returned from the hospital. She bounced and danced and spun in circles. She seemed to have stopped throwing up. At least for now.

Kyle came in behind her and shut the door. He lifted Emily out of her arms and held her against his chest. "Welcome home."

Melissa didn't know if he'd said it to her, or to Emily, or to both of them. It made them a family, in their house now. As much of a family as they might ever be.

There were streamers and balloons in the living room. She saw them and smiled. "You?"

"I had some help."

She walked into the nursery, then into their bedroom. "I'm ready to lie down again. Surprise, surprise."

Kyle came in with her. He sat down on the chair beside the bed, Emily cradled in his arms.

Melissa watched him. "What's the smile for?"

Kyle looked up from Emily. "Imagining her as a teenager."

"She'll be beautiful."

"With three rings in an eyebrow and a pin through her nose," he added, mischievous.

"Oh, God. I hope not."

"We'll love her anyway," Kyle promised.

"We will, won't we." As she said the words, she felt a soothing confidence come over her. They would be okay. All three of them.

"Yes," Kyle said.

"Even if we don't love each other we can still be a family."

"Go to sleep," Kyle said after a long moment. "I'll look after Emily."

ANITA CAME OVER LATER, and Kyle went out to play basketball. He was alone on the court, and that was how he wanted it.

He took shots. Moving slow. Feeling like an old man.

He stepped back for a three-pointer. The ball arced high, floating…and hit the rim with a clang, bouncing toward the corner of the court.

He walked after it.

He thought of what Melissa had just said. *Even if we don't love each other…* It wasn't the only time she'd noted that they didn't love each other. He didn't know why she was so insistent about it.

What the hell was love, anyway? Infatuation, neediness, vulnerability.

He remembered the broken feeling after Felicity had died. The emptiness when his dad was gone.

They had left when they couldn't stand it anymore. Kyle was too smart not to see the common thread.

He wouldn't leave. Refused absolutely to leave. However, that didn't mean he wasn't going to get left.

But as long as Melissa waited eighteen or twenty years, he told himself, then it wouldn't matter.

His shot smacked the rim.

TWO WEEKS AFTER Emily came home from the hospital, Melissa realized she'd gotten used to the fear. Somehow in the commotion of taking care of her newborn, with the nighttime feedings and the lack of sleep and the hormonal changes, the fear had settled into an almost comfortable place.

Like a talisman around her neck. There. Present. But not impeding her functions.

Instead of going to her father's house for Sunday dinner, everyone came to them. Anita and Troy ordered a take-out meal of salad, roast chicken and potatoes. They brought it over and served it up while Melissa chatted with her father and Emily.

As they began the meal, eating casually in the living room, Anita said, "We have an announcement."

"We're getting married," said Troy.

"Oh, you guys," Melissa said. "That's terrific."

"And in case you're wondering, Dad," Anita added with a smile, "I'm not pregnant. Yet."

Ben Lopez smiled back. "I'm glad to hear that. Though it wouldn't really matter. I've gotten used to things happening in the wrong order."

"When will the wedding be?" Kyle asked.

"July, maybe. We need a bit of time to pull it together, even though it won't be anything fancy."

Anita and Troy left soon after dinner. While Kyle cleaned up, Melissa and her father talked more.

She said, "You don't still think the miscarriage was your fault, do you, Dad?"

He waited a while before answering. "I still wish I'd behaved differently. It's been on my mind a lot. I realized your mother wouldn't have acted the way I did. She would have been happy for Anita, all the way through. Happy she found Troy. Happy she moved in with him. Happy she was pregnant by him, even if they weren't married. It's a different world now than it was when we were young. I think she would have adjusted better than I have."

"You've adjusted fine, Dad."

Another silence. "Your mother had a miscarriage, you know."

Melissa almost thought she hadn't heard him right. Her father rarely talked about her mother, and he'd never told her anything like that before. "No, I didn't know. When?" she asked.

"Before your sister was born."

"An early miscarriage? Like Anita's?"

He nodded. "It was before the eighth week. We were just married. Money was tight. We argued sometimes."

"She miscarried after an argument?"

He nodded. "When I came back from work it had started."

Melissa tried to digest the information she'd just received. It was hard to think of her parents arguing at all. Their household had always been very tranquil and loving.

Had her father been feeling guilty for this for over thirty years? That was crazy.

"I don't think you caused that one, either."

"Maybe not," he admitted. "But I've carried the guilt with me for a long time."

"It sounds as if Mom took it pretty hard."

"She did."

Watching his face, she said, "You don't have to answer this if you don't want to, but did you guys argue often? I was never aware of it. I was pretty young, though."

A long time passed before he answered. "Sometimes we did—sometimes we didn't. We tried to shield you kids from it."

"Every couple has disagreements, Dad."

He exhaled. "We had one the day your mother died."

"Oh, Dad." She could read on his face that he

blamed himself for that, too. "Dad, that was definitely not your fault." Her voice hitched as she said the words, put the emphasis on *definitely.*

"I always thought she might have been distracted by our fight, might have been able to avoid the truck otherwise."

"Dad, that is *not* what happened." The details of that day had been permanently seared onto her eight-year-old brain. "You should have asked me. I could have told you that a long time ago."

"I didn't want to remind you. I didn't want to make you relive it."

The way I've been reliving it for twenty-three years.

"Dad, you should have talked to me."

She took a deep breath. Since they were having an honest discussion, there was something else they needed to talk about. The truth was hard, as she'd learned in telling Kyle and Anita about the accident. But it sometimes brought relief.

"I knew how you felt after she died," she said.

Her father met her eyes. He seemed to be questioning her, asking her if she really meant what she'd said.

"I knew you contemplated suicide." She said it softly, with love.

His face seemed to crack. She saw his eyes grow wet. "Oh, honey," he said. "I never meant for you to know that."

He came over to her chair and knelt beside her

so he could put his arms around her. "Oh, God. Melissa. You never should have known that."

"I—" Her voice broke. "I overheard you one day. Talking...to her. You didn't know I was home."

"I wish you'd talked to me," he said. "There were some days I missed her so much I wanted to die, but I never would have done that to you and your sister. Never."

Not even if I deserved it? she thought. *Not even if I deserved to lose you after the pain I'd given you by taking her away?*

In the back of her mind she heard Kyle's voice. *It wasn't your fault.*

And for the first time she almost believed him.

No, she realized, she did believe him. She'd been eight years old. It hadn't been her fault.

Something had changed in her since she'd told Kyle and her sister about the accident. Now that she was no longer keeping a secret, she didn't have to cling to her feelings of guilt.

Melissa felt a wave of peacefulness sweep into her. A profound sense of relief.

"I've always thought the accident was my fault," she told her father. "I've always blamed myself."

And she told him what had happened.

FROM BESIDE EMILY'S CRIB, Kyle listened to Melissa's soft voice as she explained her feelings to her father. He wanted to go to her and hold her, but he knew this was their time together.

He'd been waiting months for her to break through to the realization she'd just had. Months.

Her courage impressed him. Made him incredibly proud.

Her father's talk about his suicide had made him think about Felicity. About people who left.

Some people, he guessed, were just the leaving type. Some people just didn't have the stamina to stick around, whether it was in a family or in life.

But not Melissa, he realized. Melissa was strong. Melissa would never skip out on her family. Not on her father and Anita. And not on Emily.

And not on him.

May

FIVE WEEKS after the birth, Melissa went in for her follow-up exam.

She strapped Emily into the car seat and got behind the wheel. This was her first time out alone since Emily's birth and it felt oddly like an adventure. There were times when she missed the freedom of being able to go wherever she wanted without all the worries of the past ten months.

The checkup with Natalie Porter went smoothly. "You've healed up beautifully," the doctor said. "Everything is almost back to normal. How are things with Emily?"

"Great," she said, not mentioning her feelings of fear. "She's a darling."

"She looks it. Milk production okay? Any discomfort from nursing?"

"Everything's okay."

"Good. You're fine to start back at work in a couple of weeks when your leave is up. I hear the E.R. has missed you. And," she added with a little wink, "you should feel free to resume your sex life any time you like."

That last bit of news was only somewhat encouraging.

After her appointment with Dr. Porter, Melissa decided to take Emily down to the E.R. to show her around. A few of her closer friends from the hospital had stopped by the house, but that was it.

Her arrival caused a stir. Everyone was happy to see her and oohed and aahed over Emily.

Her boss, Dr. Marchison, took a look at her. "You seem to have had a productive time off."

She smiled. "Yes. I certainly have."

"When do we get you back on the job? A couple of weeks, now, isn't it?" He looked down at Emily. "Though I see we have some competition for your affections. You're not going to ditch us in favor of this little charmer, are you?"

"I'll be back," she assured him. Medicine and the emergency room had been a part of her life too long for her to consider giving them up. They were a source of stability for her, a challenge and something that soothed her in a way she didn't fully understand. At least when she was successful...

WITH HER PHYSICAL HEALTH checked out, Melissa felt comfortable going ahead with their trip to the East Coast, which they had been planning since they'd announced the baby's imminent arrival to Kyle's family.

They flew nonstop to Boston and were picked up at the airport by Kyle's mother. Emily was a perfect traveler, snoozing contentedly through most of the flight and playing on Kyle's lap for the rest of the time.

Kyle's brother met them at his mother's house. The two expressed a gratifying amount of awe at Emily and then let Kyle and Melissa put her to bed. Melissa was exhausted from traveling and followed Emily to bed soon afterward, though Kyle stayed up talking with his brother and mother.

In the morning they spent time in the house with Kyle's mom, then took Emily out for a walk through Boston. It was May and the weather was perfect. The trees all had thick coats of mint-green spring leaves. Everything was clean and bright. Tulips and irises were out everywhere. Kyle and Melissa walked through the Boston Common looking at flowers and people and the resident swans.

They saw Craig and his kids the next morning. Danny and Mira were somewhat intrigued by little Emily, but their attention wasn't caught all that long by an infant so young. Emily didn't do quite enough interacting to suit them.

Melissa, though, watched the older children in fascination, and imagined her own daughter at their ages.

Around midday Kyle's mother went out to an appointment, so they had the house to themselves for a while.

"I have a project," Kyle said. "I left some things in boxes here when I moved to Portland. I think it's time to clear them out of the garage. Check through them to make sure I don't want any of the stuff and give the rest to Goodwill."

"Mmm. Sounds fun," she said, smiling.

"Hey, I never said you had to help. I was thinking you and Emily could sit near the garage and enjoy the sunshine."

"Or just keep you company while you work..."

"Right."

He got her a chair from the back patio and set it up near the open garage door in a little patch of sunlight. Melissa shaded Emily in a big white bonnet and sat with her, watching Kyle work.

He went through the boxes efficiently. None of the clothes or other items had seen the light of day in six years.

He put most of the clothes in a pile to be given away, but hung on to several items of sentimental value. "My high-school yearbook," he said, holding it out to her.

Melissa flipped through it, recognizing Kyle in several of the pictures. So *young*.

At one point Kyle pulled out a black leather jacket. "Whoa, get a load of this. I'd forgotten all about it."

It was a biker jacket, with chains and studs and heavy zippers.

Melissa stared at it. "Kyle, I never knew…"

"A total fake," Kyle explained. "One hundred percent vinyl. A gag gift from Mom. I used to wear it for Halloween sometimes."

"Put it on," she challenged.

Kyle reluctantly donned it. In the spring and fall he wore a brown leather jacket, in which he looked quite good. This was something else entirely. Way over the top.

He struck a tough pose. Melissa laughed.

"Wait," he said, and dug into one of the pockets. He extracted a pair of cheap sunglasses and put them on.

"Nice, Kyle."

"Yeah." He dropped them on the pile of stuff to give away.

At one point, while she was reading comments written by friends in his yearbook, she saw him open a box, pull out a white sweater, sized for a small woman, then refold it and return it back to the box.

Something he didn't want to deal with now. Or

something he didn't want to deal with in front of her. Things that belonged to Felicity?

She didn't ask and he didn't seem to want to talk about it. He moved right on to another box, from which he removed a scuffed black belt. "Why on earth did I keep *this?*" he asked, tossing it, too, on the pile to give away.

CHAPTER NINETEEN

MELISSA WANTED TO KNOW what was in the box.

She was even tempted, a couple of hours later, to sneak into the garage and take a look for herself, but she realized she could never do that. It was an invasion of privacy. The kind of thing she wouldn't want her daughter to witness.

Far better, she thought, to handle her curiosity honestly.

But what could you say to your husband? *I want to know about your dead fiancée so I can understand why you don't love me. Tell me what you kept of hers, so that I know what I'm up against.*

Ridiculous.

When she'd first started volunteering at the clinic Kyle had been working there ten months, and his fiancée's suicide was common knowledge among the staff and doctors. No one mentioned it to his face, of course, and he didn't talk about it.

But he was aware people knew. The first time he'd mentioned it to her had been two years into their friendship, in the summer, when he was having a particularly hard week. He'd said to her, "You know about Felicity, right?"

And she'd nodded. There was no point playing coy; that wasn't the kind of friendship they were developing.

"It happened around this time of year," he'd said.

Around this time of year.

As if he wouldn't remember the exact date, the very hour, only three years earlier. Melissa's heart had gone out to him. She'd understood how it was to not want to talk about something.

Now, having seen that box in the garage, she couldn't help needing to know more. To see what had drawn him to Felicity.

The woman he had actually *wanted* to marry.

LATER THAT AFTERNOON Melissa took Emily to their bedroom to nurse. They were staying in the room Kyle had lived in when he was young.

On his bookshelf was a photo album. She took it down and perched it on her lap while Emily fed.

She turned the pages slowly, seeing Kyle and his brother and mother in various pictures during his growing-up years. A grade-school play. Days at the beach, a ski vacation.

There were blank spaces on the pages where photos seemed to have been removed. Not hard to guess who had been in them.

She found it poignant to see Kyle in the different stages of his life. After a prolonged awkward stretch in the early teenaged years the adult Kyle started to emerge.

She guessed he was quite a heartthrob during high school. But that wasn't too much of a guess. Many of the notes in his yearbook had been in rounded female handwriting, with circles to dot the *I*s.

In the back of the photo album she found an unsealed envelope. With her free hand she opened it and pulled out a small stack of photos.

The ones that had been removed from the album. The ones with Kyle's father in them.

The resemblance between the two was uncanny. The pictures looked as if they could have been of Kyle but for the hairstyle and the clothes. In most of them, Kyle's father was around the same age as Kyle was now.

Melissa was still looking at them when Kyle came into the room.

He saw what she was doing, but she couldn't tell what his reaction was. "Sorry," she said. "I'm prying."

"It's okay."

"You resemble him a lot."

"I'm not like him."

"I know you're not."

He stood for a moment, as if making a decision. "There's something else I want to show you. I'll be right back."

KYLE WENT TO THE GARAGE and got the box of Felicity's things. On the way back to the bedroom he stopped in his mother's home office for her microcassette recorder.

He brought the things into his old bedroom. Emily still nursed at Melissa's breast. The sight of it never ceased to amaze him.

"She's a hungry little one," he said.

Melissa was eyeing the box. "Are those Felicity's things?"

"Yes."

"I saw you open the box earlier," she said.

"I didn't know if you had."

"I've been curious," she admitted.

"Of course. I'm sure I would have felt the same way."

He pulled apart the flaps of the box.

"You kept these things," Melissa said.

"Initially I kept them. Then I just had them. And then I never knew what to do with them."

The sweater was the first thing to come out. He held it up, remembering how Felicity had looked in it one day at the zoo. It had been a good day. Happy.

"Tell me about her," Melissa said.

He did so. Felicity had been blond, small boned, and classically beautiful. She'd worked as a copywriter at a Boston advertising firm.

As he spoke about her, in a way he hadn't to anyone in over six years, he pulled other items from the box. "She'd left these at my apartment," he said.

They reminded him of the woman he'd known, the one who'd been alive, who'd seemed happy on the surface, glad to be marrying him.

In the bottom of the box, underneath all the other items, was the microcassette.

Kyle thought about that day.

Felicity, dead.

Stillness.

Melissa asked, "What's on the tape?"

He'd brought the cassette recorder upstairs for just this purpose, knowing he would have to listen to the tape one last time. This tape, which had haunted him in the days after her death…

He got the machine from his bag. "Her answering-machine tape," he explained. Hers had been one of the inexpensive kinds of machines with only one tape. The outgoing message was at the beginning, followed by any incoming messages.

Kyle pressed Play.

"Hi, we can't come to the phone right now, but leave a message and we'll call you back."

Felicity's voice. Her own tones and rhythms. Something no one else had, no one could replicate. Utterly hers.

And gone.

She sounded like a stranger to him. Someone he'd hardly known.

There was a pause. Then his own voice came on. Younger. Innocent. Unaware. "Hey, Felicity. Just phoning to check in. Call me this afternoon, okay? I'll see you at six for dinner."

Another pause.

His voice again. A second message. "Still out, huh? Okay. I'll see you later."

He hadn't phoned again.

At six he'd rung her doorbell. Waited, then let himself in with her key.

She'd been on the bed.

Cold in the air-conditioned room.

He'd called 911 anyway, and the double strobe of the answering machine had taunted him while he gave the address.

He'd listened to the messages while he'd waited. Heard his own voice.

The messages hadn't been played. She hadn't gotten his calls because he'd waited until after lunch to call her. He had replayed the messages again after the ambulance and the police had left. His voice, unconcerned, reaching out to her as if nothing was wrong.

Too late.

By the time he'd called she'd already died. Or was she on her way, the pills at work in her system? Had she heard the phone ring? Heard his voice and recognized it? Wanted to answer but been unable?

Or had his message only confirmed her decision?

Better to think she'd already died. Easier that way.

It was like wondering what might have happened if he'd called earlier. It could have saved her, or it could have changed nothing. And he would never know.

"She didn't get the messages," he said.

Melissa didn't need the explanation. He saw tears on her cheeks.

He removed the cassette and set it on the pile of items. There were a few more things in the bottom of the box. Two advertisements torn from newspapers. A funny one for a new store opening in Harvard Square. A more serious one for the transit authority.

Melissa read them. "She was good."

"She was." It added to the things that didn't make sense. Like his father leaving his family.

The last item in the box was a picture of the two of them. Him and Felicity arm in arm. Similar to the one he'd kept in Portland. She looked happy, but it hadn't been true.

He looked happy, too, but he just hadn't known the truth.

He put the picture down on the pile of stuff. Turned to his wife.

"It's hard when people die," she said. "There's nothing left."

He thought of Melissa at eight years of age, losing her mother. "Felicity must have known I would find her."

"She might not have been thinking that clearly."

"Yeah."

"She shouldn't have done it."

"No."

"Not to you, and not to her family. And not to herself. There is nothing," she said, fierce, "*nothing* in this world that's worth killing yourself over."

Quiet. He peered at the picture on top of the stack. "I wouldn't know you if things had been different. I wouldn't have Emily."

Bittersweet. Not looking at her.

"Neither would I."

Stillness.

Quiet, neither of them looking at each other.

Before they'd left Portland he'd realized Melissa would never leave him as Felicity had. That knowledge had opened up something inside him. Released something he'd been holding on to much too tightly.

"What am I going to do with this stuff?"

"Keep it, if you want. We've got room."

"I don't want it," he said. It was time to move on, to put the past behind him, and that didn't include hanging on to Felicity's clothing. Still, it was hard just to get rid of someone's things when that was all she'd left behind.

"Give it to Goodwill."

He nodded. It was the best option. At least the money from selling the clothes would cycle around to people who needed it.

"It's okay," she said. "You loved her."

"Did I?"

He didn't know anymore.

THAT EVENING THEY DROVE up to the North Shore for a lobster dinner in a run-down lobster shack. Melissa loved it. The food was delicious—buttery and smooth and rich. They washed it down with tall glasses of soda, then walked around outside to enjoy the spring night.

She felt closer to Kyle after his openness with her. It helped to know about Felicity. To see that he had been able to put her behind him.

Kyle's mom, a sure and experienced driver, was at the wheel on the way home.

They were only a few blocks from the house when the accident happened.

CHAPTER TWENTY

MELISSA WATCHED IT HAPPEN as if in slow motion.

A sports-utility vehicle traveling beside them down the surface artery swerved right into them, sideswiping their car and sending it toward a line of parked cars.

Kyle's mom fought for control. She managed to miss the cars, but their car went into a skid, fishtailed briefly, then abruptly turned around before coming to a ragged halt only a few feet from a lamppost. Vehicles honked, but they had stopped clear of any intersections.

Melissa sat in the back seat, next to Emily in her car seat.

Panic struck, hard.

She'd been feeling so good a few minutes earlier. So confident. Now that was gone.

She tried to keep breathing regularly, to remind herself that she was okay, that Emily appeared to be unhurt.

Both Kyle and his mom were asking if she was okay.

She felt as if time had stopped, as if she couldn't

get a grip on reality, and she heard herself saying, "I don't know," over and over.

WHILE THEY WAITED for the police to arrive, Kyle stood on the sidewalk with his arms around Melissa. She was shaking and she refused to let go of Emily, but she was unharmed.

Physically.

The sense of relief when the accident had ended and he'd realized none of them had been hurt had been overwhelming.

The sense of relief that *Melissa* hadn't been hurt.

After the police and tow truck had arrived and the formalities were done, Kyle got everyone into a taxicab and home.

Once there, he followed Melissa to their room.

"I need to feed Emily," she said. Her voice sounded flat, as it had ever since the accident. She sat in the chair by the window. "You don't need to stay," she told him.

She unbuttoned her blouse and held Emily up to her breast, cradling her. All her attention went to the infant.

"I'm glad you're both safe," Kyle said.

Melissa didn't respond.

SHE FELT BETTER in the morning. Not quite as shaken. She picked up Emily and hugged her to her breast.

Her daughter was just fine. Unhurt.

This time.

The fear she'd felt at the hospital hadn't been for nothing, she thought. It was exactly this that she'd been afraid of, even if the accident had been only a reminder of the possibility of loss.

They had been incredibly lucky. Unbelievably lucky. But that didn't mean they would be lucky the next time.

In the long night she'd thought of all the awful things that happened to children. Fevers, abductions, schoolyard shootings. Kids beaten and left to die on fence posts just because they were gay. Traffic accidents, muggings, murders. The world was a dangerous place.

But nothing could change the fact that Emily was in it. She deserved Melissa's unconditional love no matter what might happen to her. That was a price Melissa was willing to pay.

To withhold love from a child just because you were afraid of losing her... That was criminal.

Kyle was another story.

Her love for him was different. Not unconditional, but selfish and greedy. She had learned to turn to him. He had made it possible to stop living alone with her guilt over the accident with her mother. He had made it possible for her forgive herself.

And the thought of losing him...

It was too much to contemplate.

She couldn't keep loving him. She couldn't set herself up for that kind of pain.

SOMETHING HAD CHANGED, Kyle realized. He'd thought they were slowly breaking down the wall between them. Sharing the tasks of taking care of Emily had brought them closer to each other.

Melissa was withdrawn and flat with him the rest of that evening and for the next day. With Emily she was an attentive mother, and she made an effort to be polite to Kyle's mom, who was a little rattled by the accident herself. But she seemed to treat Kyle as if he were a stranger.

The life had gone out of their visit to Boston.

Kyle knew she was upset about the car accident. That it had made her remember losing her mother and her brother.

That didn't make it any easier to have her treat him this way.

KYLE TOLD HIS MOTHER about the car accident Melissa had experienced when she was eight years old.

"How awful," his mother said. "Our accident the other night must have been very traumatic for her."

"It was."

"It's natural to pull back when the world is too hard to deal with."

"I know."

"But that doesn't make it any easier to watch the person you love go through that."

"No," he said, automatically agreeing with her.

"Especially when you love someone as much as you love Melissa."

Kyle's vision blurred.

His mother believed that they were in love with each other. Just as he wanted her to.

But as the words echoed in his head, he realized they were true.

…when you love someone as much as you love Melissa.   What he felt for Melissa wasn't the kind of emotion you felt for your friend, even your best friend.

She was his wife, not just some partner in an arrangement.

He loved her, after all.

The fact of it didn't shock him, only that he hadn't realized it sooner. It was like something he'd known for a long time but just hadn't tried to verbalize. Like a familiar friend…

He loved her.

While she, of course, had made it clear she felt nothing but friendship for him. This, he realized, was why he had felt something missing in their lovemaking. Because on some level he had known that he wanted their lovemaking to be about *love*, not about sex.

He loved her.

And he didn't know what the hell to do about it.

HE THOUGHT THINGS between them might get better when they returned to Portland. When she was in her own house, and possibly feeling more secure.

They didn't.

She was a perfect mother. She gave Emily every ounce of love she could.

There was nothing for him. No more than casual friendship. The way their relationship had been in the beginning, when they'd hardly known each other.

She was nice to him.

Nice.

Kyle didn't want *nice*. He wanted a wife. A life partner. Someone who loved him as much as he loved her.

KYLE TRIED TO BE PATIENT.

It taxed him to the limit. He found out that when it came to love, he just wasn't a patient person.

One day when the house was quiet and Emily was sleeping happily in her crib, he went and found Melissa in the kitchen. She sat at the kitchen table with a mug of tea and a medical journal.

When he walked in she said, ''Hi, Kyle,'' but she went right back to reading.

He pulled up the chair opposite her. "We need to talk."

She finished her paragraph and closed the journal. "Sure. Let's talk."

He noticed she kept her finger in the journal to mark her place. It was one of the many signals she'd been sending him. *I have a few minutes to talk with you but other things are more important to me.*

He ignored the gesture and how it made him feel.

"I don't like the way our relationship is going."

She looked at him as if she honestly had no idea what he was talking about. "What's not to like? We're friends and we love our daughter. It's just as we planned."

"Friends share things. They enjoy life together. They do more than just inhabit the same physical space."

She smiled at him. "I'll try to share more."

She said it without any sarcasm, as if he had really reached her and she was willing to change.

He didn't buy it.

"I understand why you're sometimes scared of close relationships," he said. "Especially since you lived through such an awful experience when you were younger. You lost two people you loved deeply, and I know you don't want to have to go through that again."

"True," she said.

"I know our accident was hard for you."

''It was just a fender bender, Kyle. I was a bit shaken up, but it's no big deal.''

At her words, so clearly false, everything clicked into place. He was surprised he hadn't seen it before.

Her repeated declarations that they had married for friendship rather than love.

That inane analysis—the morning after they'd first made love again—of a supposed male ability to have friendly sex without deeper feeling.

Her abrupt withdrawal from him after their recent accident.

They could mean only one thing. She loved him.

If she didn't love him, if she hadn't been in love with him for a while, just as he had been in love with her, then why would she bother to push him away?

She *must* love him.

He met her eyes. ''You can't stop loving people because of fear. Love doesn't work that way.''

''Whatever, Kyle.''

He risked it. ''You won't stop loving *me,* either, just because you're afraid.''

She was silent for an excruciatingly long time. ''I don't love you,'' she said at last.

It had the ring of truth. It sounded like a harsh confession from someone who didn't want to have to break the bad news but who knew her feelings would never change.

Kyle smelled a rat.

"That's too bad," he said. "Because I love you."

He watched her, trying to gauge her reaction. There was none, as far as he could tell.

"It took me a while to realize it, but I love you. We crossed the bridge from friendship a long time ago, maybe even before we slept together. But I've been holding myself back, unconsciously, afraid of losing you. Afraid of what happened with Felicity and my father."

She had her eyes closed now, and he couldn't tell if she was pretending not to listen or was bored.

"But our accident made me realize something. It reminded me that life is risky. People get sick. Have accidents. Die. You love people even knowing that you might lose them, that they might be snatched away from you. Because the only other option, as attractive as it seems right now, is untenable. We've both tried living without love. But it doesn't work. So you have to take the risk."

Melissa's eyes opened. "Risk," she said. "What do you know about risk?

He said, "Damn it, Melissa. Losing people by accident I can live with. I understand that now. But a deliberate choice to leave me is something else entirely. My father did that to me. Felicity did that to me."

Even Blue's parents had done it to him, though Blue had been the one to leave. But Zita hadn't run away. She'd taken on the full risk of loving another being, and Kyle suspected she had been happier in her last months than she had been in many years.

That was worth something.

"Now *you* want to do that to me, Melissa. You're trying to leave me now, to erase the love we have for each other so it won't hurt so much if I'm not around anymore. But I won't let you do it."

"You can't stop someone from leaving. You should know that, Kyle. You of all people."

The words were meant to wound. They did, but he let the hurt wash out of him.

"You're trying to stop me from loving you," he told her. "And it's not going to work. I promise you, it's not going to work. I won't stop loving you. And I won't ever leave you. Not by choice."

She was silent. Absolutely still. He noticed her finger no longer held her place in the medical journal.

Something relaxed inside him. He could breathe again.

"You do love me, don't you?"

She looked away. It was a long time before she answered. "I don't want to."

"That's a yes."

She said nothing.

"Melissa, look at me. That's a yes, isn't it?"

"Yes." It was only a whisper.

"Say it, then. Tell me you love me."

She met his gaze. He could see the sheen of tears in her eyes. "I love you."

He pushed his chair back and went to her. He knelt on the floor beside her chair and hugged her.

The contact was different than ever before. Her body was right there against his. She wasn't holding anything back. There was no wall between them. "Melissa, help me make this marriage a real one."

He felt her nod her head on his shoulder. His face was buried in her hair and it smelled like gardenia. "Is that a yes?"

"Yes."

He hugged her more tightly. "It'll be scary sometimes."

"I know."

"We'll be in it together."

Melissa pulled back and looked into Kyle's eyes. Letting herself be there with him. Completely. "I love you," she said.

And then they were kissing.

She didn't know who started it, and she didn't care.

HEART OF THE WEST

Every Man Has His Price!

Lost Springs Ranch was
famous for turning young
mavericks into good men.
So word that the ranch was
in financial trouble sent
a herd of loyal bachelors
stampeding back to
Wyoming to put themselves
on the auction block!

July 1999	**Husband for Hire** Susan Wiggs	January 2000	**The Rancher and the Rich Girl** Heather MacAllister
August	**Courting Callie** Lynn Erickson	February	**Shane's Last Stand** Ruth Jean Dale
September	**Bachelor Father** Vicki Lewis Thompson	March	**A Baby by Chance** Cathy Gillen Thacker
October	**His Bodyguard** Muriel Jensen	April	**The Perfect Solution** Day Leclaire
November	**It Takes a Cowboy** Gina Wilkins	May	**Rent-a-Dad** Judy Christenberry
December	**Hitched by Christmas** Jule McBride	June	**Best Man in Wyoming** Margot Dalton

HARLEQUIN®
Makes any time special ™